FAMILY ROMANCE

visuals by
NICK PATTERSON

verbals by
TOM BRADLEY

FAMILY ROMANCE

visuals by Nick Patterson
verbals by Tom Bradley

Jaded Ibis Press
sustainable literature by digital means™
an imprint of Jaded Ibis Productions U.S.A.

Now go and smite the Amalekites,
and utterly destroy all that they have,
and spare them not; but slay both
man and woman, infant and suckling,
ox and sheep, camel and ass.
—1 Samuel 15:3

i.

"Cover your face with both hands when you sneeze. You never know when a pathogen has fastened on your head."

That's Mom talking. As usual she's forcing herself on us and in us. She must control our reflex motions. Mom must micro-manage the gases and moisture that exit our faces. She gets fidgety and unfulfilled unless occupying other creatures' sinuses and limbs, the gluttoness.

I object to being mothered by a creature so ravenous (if intermittently shapely). And I'm sure my dear siblette would agree, if the sad child were still able to mull more than half a notion inside what remains of her mind.

As for the more explicitly testicular of our parents—who knows where absent Dad would come down on this issue? Mom and pathogens are the sole topics he refuses to discuss in secret letters from across the Judeuphrates, where has defected to please himself behaving like a traitor/apostate among the Relic Amalekites.

In Dad's absence, Mom's favorite way to rape us of self-possession is immune system anxiety. She has taken the germ theory and twisted it into pre-moistened masochist porn. Her term for any well-being threat is "pathogen."

Not just bacteria and viruses, not merely lice and tapeworms, but psychosomatosis, connective tissue sprain, clinical depression, poor social connectivity, sulphurous flatulence, scrotal and/or labial fatigue from excessive "maestrobation" (as she taught us to mispronounce it)—all of these are brought on by pathogens. This is according to the fascist conjuress whom we are expected to call, for lack of a less inappropriate moniker, Mom.

And yet, in spite of the pan-systemic pathogens that lurk everywhere, Mom was somehow persuaded (presumably by Dad) to grunt me out into this world, and to perform the same disservice for my emotionally vegetative little sissy. One after the other, Mom extruded the pair of us. She dragged our naked spirits down from the gritty smog overhead and enfleshed us, emboned us, left us to languish dadlessly on the planetary crust, bug-vulnerable and liable at any moment to succumb to—

the Sneeze Catastrophic—

Mom dresses us in
off-the-shoulder love-sarongs.

You won't be surprised to hear that Mom prettifies her pathogens before siccing them on us. Such organisms are too precious to flit around in plain brown wrappers. A typical Mom-bug will boast not only feathery antennae, but glamorous pseudo-eyes on its wings. In much the same way our practitioners of municipal priestcraft will tart themselves up in the whole-body spandex chasuble before yanking felonious blasphemers' armpits inside-out. Little Sister once fell afoul of the priestcrafters, and she could tell you all about the dread civil/sacral strappado if she were able to mouth more than a half-dozen baby words these days.

The maternal instinct in our remaining parent is not so much atrophied as sarcastic. She prettifies us, too, just like her pet sick-makers. Even in this epoch of worldly war and widespread privation, Mom somehow scrounges the means to bring about lovely coiffures high upon our occupied heads, all the better for her unwellness vectors to perch and nest. She gussies us up in off-the-shoulder love-sarongs, thick in fiber, subtropical in batik.

I don't know about my sweet little siblette's love-sarong, but it seems likely the weft of my particular garment has an ulterior warp.

All moms want their non-girlish offspring to cling like an acetate nightie to sex-wet thighs. And, if you are a canny mom, you know the best way to promote clinginess is to live in a neighborhood where something strange happens every time your non-girl slips out to perform the backyard chores.

ii.

I am expected each dawn, noon and dusk to go out and gather our calories. This is an atavism from our former registered status as Military Family. The eldest spawn of a Ceremonial Cavalryman is the designated forager, according to martial/canonical law as divinely revealed in those glorious days before whatever was going on a long time ago supposedly happened.

When I say we are—rather, before the paternal abandonment, were—a Military Family, I wonder if it's possible to emphasize strongly enough the extent and depth to which the quartet of us once fit into that relatively lofty caste.

I suppose the starting question should be how we became a family, with a lower-case eff, in the first place. How in the name of our exclusive national/racial god, the divine Krystelle Rex, did someone so reputedly unsickish as Dad ever get infected by a syndrome of such virulent pathogens
as have been wadded together and misnomered "Mom"?

I'm told the pair met, time gone by, at—where else?—a gala defense industry expo. The venue of their first love-sighting was a vast convention center in the riverside megalopolis, within shooting distance of what was to become our dining room.

within shooting distance

Soon-to-be-Dad, still young and green in judgment, was a hereditary recruit in the ceremonial Mounted Corps. He seems to have been born with a cavalryman's plasma osmosing through his various connective tissues. This is convenient, because enrollment in that august body happens to be his inborn lot in civic/caste life.

But violence zaps through his muscles as well. This renders him unsuited for the decorative function to which the cavalry has degenerated over the millennia. Dad requested leave from his regiment to engage in warcraft—or at least vicariously to experience state sanctioned genocide via the magic of stagecraft.

So he landed a gig as a corporate mascot at the expo. In full entomo-mechano drag, on cue, he was paid to come looming and shrieking from a backlit phosphorus explosion. He promised satisfactory levels of pugnacity to bulk purchasers of a powerful biocidal agent marketed under a now-famous brand name. Here's the pitch he recited while trundling around the dais trying to look lethal:

Our product is being applied to great effect in the Middling Orient. It's specially formulated to liquefy the strange yet probably sentient rind of the Relic Amalekites, who were supposed to have been genocided like a freckle off the flaking face of the earth way back in porno-scriptural times.

The Relic Amalekites' tenaciousness is only surpassed by their furtiveness, as they make like nomads among the grit dunes of their home-sand on the perennially disputed far bank of the Judeuphrates. Our Sovereign Theocracy, under the sway of the Grand Religiopath, intends to complete the grim chore this time around, and to smite these vermin once and for all, with the help of—

(electronic rhythm-box roll...)

Flamma-Manna

Dad landed a gig as corporate mascot.

family / romance

It just occurred to me that you might get the wrong idea about Dad from the above. Shall I provide you, now, with an utterance on the same subject from this individual in his maturity?

Here's something direct and recent from his pen, as opposed to a script he memorized as a youth for a pittance. For further geopolitical background, I refer you to this secret letter which a wiser Dad dispatched from an encampment dug into the "grit dunes," camouflaged under poisoned and smoldering palm fronds. (Incidentally, I am not prepared at this point to reveal how this lethal correspondence comes before my eyes; you are free to suspect a foolhardy or suicidal postman.)

The atrophied conscience of our Sovereign Theocracy's priestcrafters, in the person of the Grand Religiopath, saw fit to unleash agony and melting death upon the Relic Amalekites' first line of defense—namely, their epidermis. Hence illiberal applications of Flamma-Manna were decreed, toward the promotional marketing of which, it mortifies me to admit, I once stumbled around in a clown suit. I am trying to make amends with saddle sores today, and bubbling skin on the more exposed parts of me.

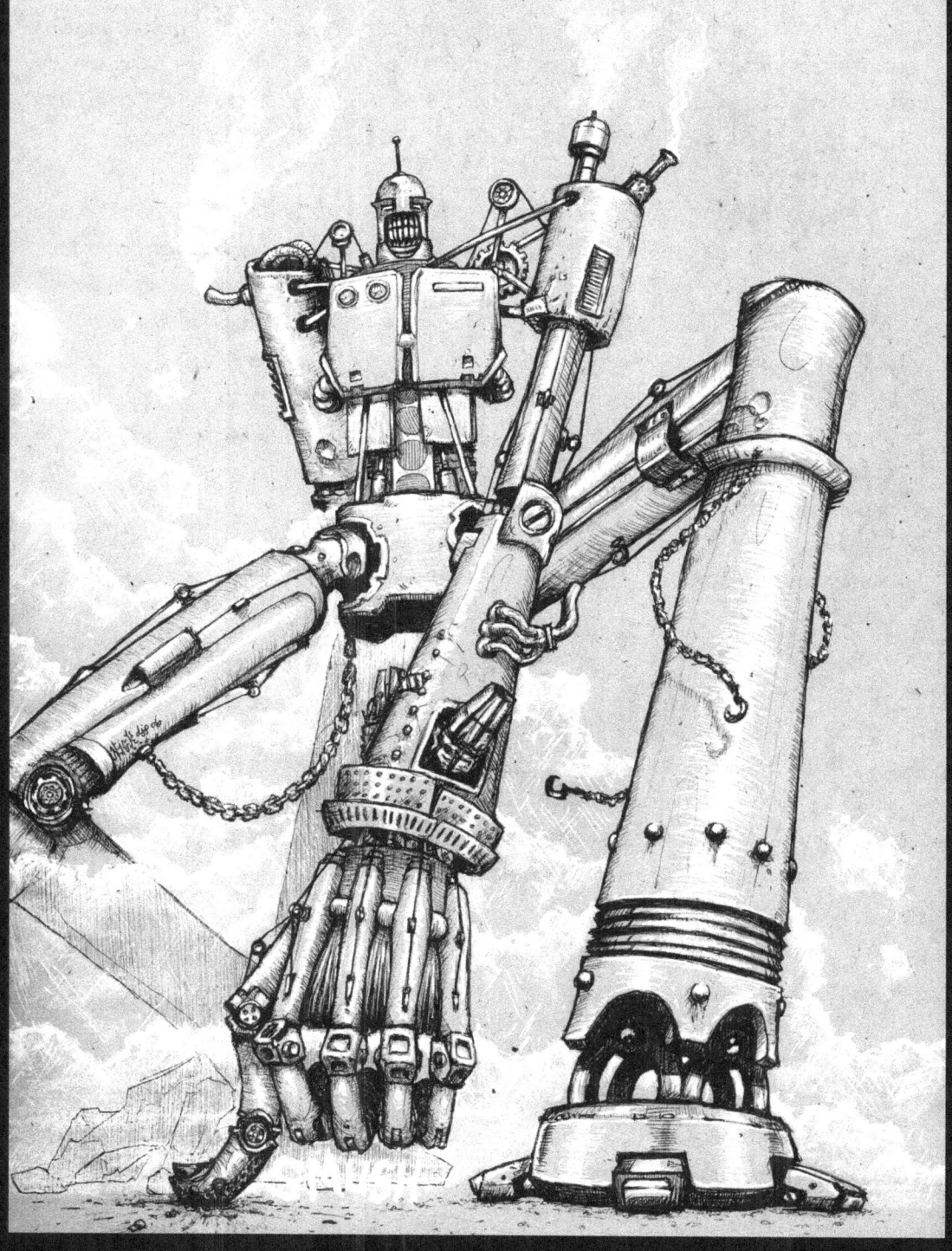

Weapon of Sparse Destruction

It floats whitely down from the sky to no pleasant effect, this Flamma-Manna, causing civilians to scurry thitherward in their huddled masses. But I, a seasoned mercenary, an 'infidel/turncoat,' am by nature obdurate enough to stick it out. I've come to enjoy the bracing sting, like a slap on the face with chilled astringent of a suburban morning.

The Grand Religiopath's justification for this biocide is that "vegetative cover needs to be removed" (it's the most barren sand in the world) to aid his search for the Relic Amalekites' notorious Weapon of Sparse Destruction. This ostensible techno-abomination is believed to be capable of long-range surgical strikes. Precision comes with the package precisely because the destruction is so sparse.

If it existed, which it certainly does not, this device would be the very definition of inefficiency. Still, that doesn't add plausibility to the ludicrous claim that it could, in a thousand years, have been developed by an ethno-species which is barely lingual, much less technological.

Might it be too cynical to suspect that the whole murderous enterprise is being dumped on my head as a marketing ploy, promo for a certain biocidal agent?

Meanwhile, back in time, at the gala defense industry expo, pre-Mom (whose attitudes toward foreigners of any stripe never mellowed with maturity) was working the punters as a double-threat taxi dancer/vintage weapons demonstratrix. In the latter role, her stage designation was—

Equestrienne Princess of the Month

Of course, only a lass of her endogamous Cavalry Caste background could qualify for such an honorific. And it seems to have suited her at the time, for she was still relatively fresh and naked in her maidenly pre-incarnation (such as it was).

As Dad lumbered about in his mascot suit, he kept one eye on this princess, and was wowed by her performance. Particularly moving was the manner in which she employed her formidable vagina as a pointing device to indicate her ride's excellent vertebral development.

Mom's formidable vagina points out
the excellence of her ride.

It was one of those quaintly dated odd-toed ungulates which were brought into being so stylishly in the bygone era, with such simple, naked pugnacity as to appeal to the sentimental hearts of all war-makers, mounted or un-. It pranced double time, this ride of Mom's, with the precision of a Lipizzan and the footedness of a Clydesdale. Dad marveled as Mom clanked on her gelding, as she cantered and pranced among the proud, pious-patriotic blood-satin bunting, a bayonet penised to her flexi-femur, a symbolically penisoid dunce cap erected on her pate, shaven for the occasion.

Their shifts over, both pretty young people having ducked behind the bunting, one of my future parents made haste to un-thigh the other from the trotter. In the process he is assumed to have blastulated the youngster who, in the future, this future, would write the romance which you presently hold in your hands, instead of keeping those organs freed up, at the ready, fingers extended, should a pathogen flutter off these colored pages and insinuate a Sneeze Catastrophic upon the frontal portion of your head.

I say Dad is assumed to have blastulated me behind the patriotic bunting. This is not my, but rather society's default assumption, Mom being my "mom" and all. I suspect virgin birth—if that's not too presumptuous. If his breath were bearable, it might be useful to consult my father's nemesis, the Grand Religiopath, on the matter.

And when, of course, in the blink of an eye, the time came for marital warfare to be waged, so inevitable in these times of regimental rot and declining troop morale, Dad not only forsook his brand-new, freely chosen wife, but he deserted his immemorially and genetically predetermined branch of the armed services. Dad abandoned the household which he'd been simultaneously born and conscripted to defend, and he turned his muscly back on our Sovereign Theocracy as well, along with its synonymous race and coextensive land mass. I believe this is called "quite a step in one's personal development."

It was the sheer excellence of Mom's demonstration that led to the loss of the very hubby she gained by it. To her chagrin, it turned out not to be herself but her ride that he hankered to centaurize onto. Some dads are driven away by their Moms. Our Dad was ridden away by himself. He became one, as they say, with the very odd-toed ungulate which Mom had vaginated so ably at the expo. (Shall we say he requisitioned it for an unspecified period of time?)

Some grooms ride their brides. Dad groomed his ride. The two of them, like a disembodied spirit and its energumen, rode to the banks of the Judeuphrates and waded across, straight into the peculiarly shaped arms whose flesh he'd helped to dissolve with his sales pitch.

Dad became one with the odd-toed ungulate.

The Relic Amalekites are among the few political entities on the planet quaint enough to maintain a mounted regiment in anything more than a decorative capacity. Seeing as how the average Relic Amalekite crotch is better adapted for squatting and shitting on the ground than hemorrhoiding on a government-issue saddle, this quaintness could be interpreted as a fine example of idiotic backwardness. It might even have something to do with how convenient our Sovereign Theocracy is finding their extermination—rather, "smiting" is the term which the Grand Religiopath says we should prefer. Sounds much more authoritative, I suppose, coming from received splatter-porno/scripture.

Regarding the absence of the person formerly known around our dining room by the three-letter capital-D word, a cynical supposition has been seeping through the riverside megalopolis. It is said that neither politics nor pity, but merely love of galloping, cantering and trotting caused Dad to skip across the river with spurs and bridle.

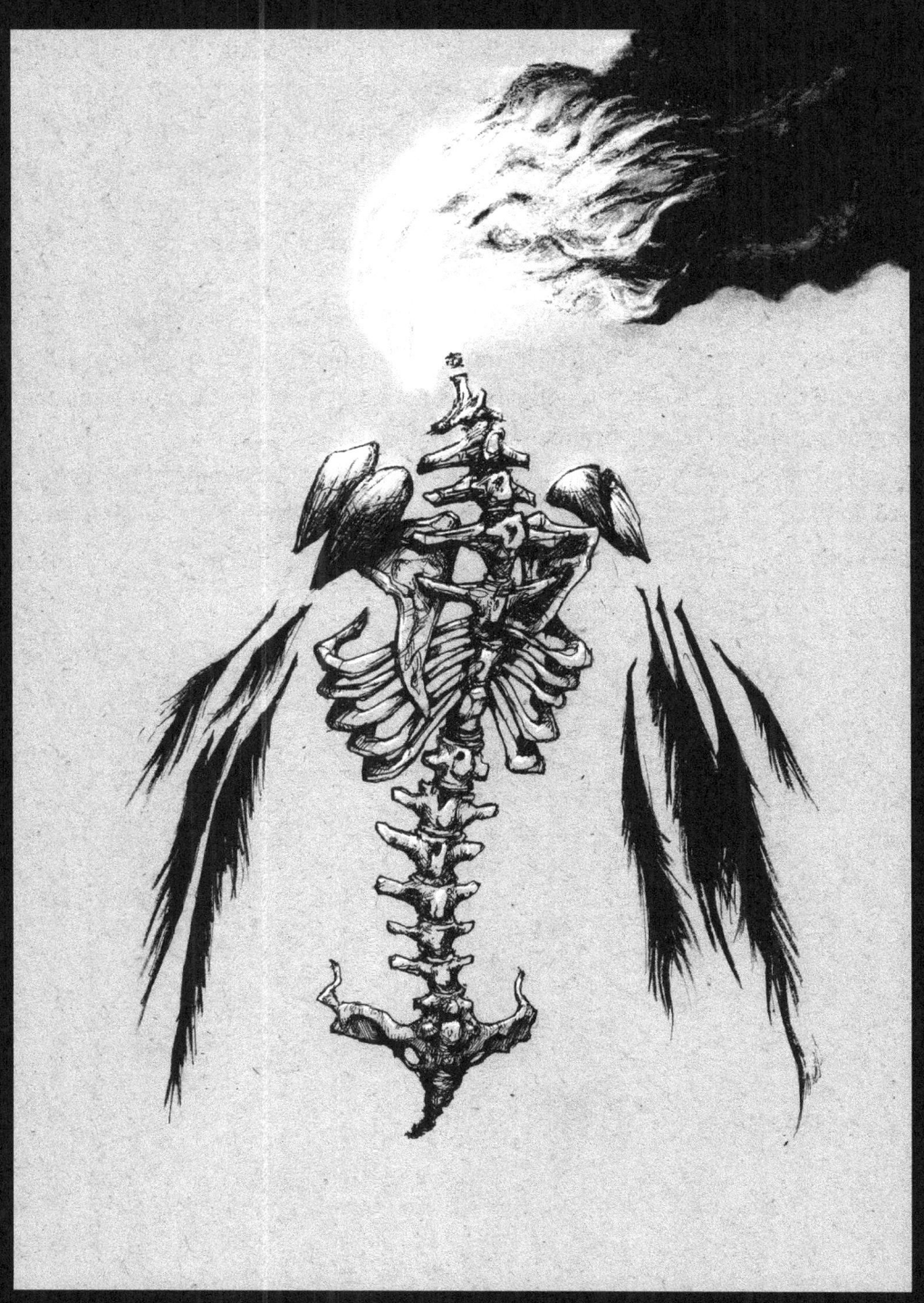

Flamma Manna floats whitely down
from the sky to no pleasant effect.

For whatever reason, Dad has exiled himself in the Middling Orient, that un-Krystelle Rexed, hence damned quadrant of our planet where no grass sprouts underfoot, just drifts of hoof-eroding minerals, jags of crystal shards, where no branchy things spring from mixed mud, because, three paces beyond the frequently dry riverbed itself, there's never ambient fluid enough to make mud, but just a monocultured desert, and precious little of the sort of fecundity that flops, red, green and fungal, from mommish pudenda.

The Relic Amalekites' Middlingly Oriental homeland is the sort of grim purgatory where, if non-girlish offspring were sent out each dawn, noon and dusk to gather calories, they would return with nothing to eat but glops of their own fingertips, melted to red Flamma-Manna-mush.

And if I, seed of an infidel and traitorous sharer of outdated military technology, still forage prior to every meal, it's for a platoon whose lieutenant was self-fragged long ago.

iii.

B esides scrounging for nutriment, I engage in another atavistic behavior thrice daily. With the mindless regularity of an autonomic nervous tic, I join my father-free family in pre-meal devotional grovels to our exclusive national-racial god—

the divine
Krystelle Rex

The exposure of our god's wormy pathogen-ridden condition appeals to Mom's religious sensibility. It's a gesture of piety on her part to dress us like him. Mom learned about the love-sarong from the divine Krystelle Rex, for he, too, was wrapped by his own problematically parthenogenic mom, and given a hermaphroditic name to go with the look.

How will he cover his face
with both hands?

"But," Mom recites by rote from Holy Writ before we dip spoons in bowls, "when the time for immolation came, the Divine Krystelle Rex was compelled, in the name of humiliation, to roll down his immaculate love-sarong. He furled it from off-the-shoulder to just-above-pubis. The exposure mortified our god more than the elbow-chains and worm-pathogens pained him. This we can tell from soberly pondering the Divine Krystelle Rex's facial expression in our certified and registered battalion-issue iconic representation—"

She holds up the graphic in question. We pause, spoons poised, soberly to meditate upon God's embarrassed facial expression. He did have a bit of a tummy on him.

Back in my little sister's long-gone lingual days, before she fell prey to this deity's clergy/bureau of priestcrafters, she would interrupt the pre-meal devotional with panicky sounds that should have forewarned us of brain disasters in the offing. In my recurring nightmare-memories of mealtimes, Sissy always shudders these words:

"God looks like he's just about to make the Sneeze Catastrophic! See how he sucks in! But how will he be able to cover his face with both—" Unable to finish her question, my beloved siblette begins to bray like a poorly bred odd-toed ungulate.

Mom ignores her younger offspring's ominous sounds and directs us to consider the divine Krystelle Rex's worms, his chains. We avert our eyes from his shamefully down-rolled love-sarong, all the while trying similarly to ignore Dad's empty stool at the head of the table.

Even if he wasn't across the river these days, he would be absent from this devotional. If I might not exactly share it, at least I can relay my father's contempt for the Divine Krystelle Rex. In one of his letters secretly dispatched from the trans-Judeuphrates, where he rides in the cavalry of a rival deity, Dad has discharged his spiritual arsenal thus:

Kryssie-poo was up to his fisty-wisties in altar boys, which doesn't say a whole lot. Do you think they chainifixed and wormolated him on no charge whatever? His mitts were cauterized at the wrist-knobs for mutual maestrobation with a minor mammaloid.

Sure, it was a time of social chaos. But guess who behaved worse than anybody. Why do you think they cooked up a spanking for li'l Missy almost as exquisite as the one I'm in for if I ever cross the Judeuphrates again?

If the Grand Religiopath ever re-corkscrewed his venomous tongue into me, it would make Krystelle Rex's iconic passion look like a junior princess-style birthday party. (Tell your siblette I can't make it this year, also.)

Sure, it was a time of social chaos, but..

Please do "soberly ponder the certified and registered facial expression" on that asinine icon your mother flaps in your face before letting you continue your slow death by malnutrition. Look at that lusty mouth on him. You can tell Miss Divine Kryssie-pooters repented at the last minute, because he was ashamed of finding his martyrdom so toothsome. That's no pre-Sneeze Catastrophic on his mug. It's a spooge-squirt gasp.

If they really wanted to punish these exhibitionistic masochists, they'd chainifix and wormolate them in a dark room rather than a major metropolitan street corner. Or they'd at least tell them to pull their love-sarongs up to modest off-the-shoulder level.

When I say, "they," of course, I mean practitioners of priestcraft, who are the same in all times and places, and under all banners, regardless of the alias, fake nose and rhinestone bathrobe they provisionally slap on the Single Universal Bloated Emanation they all serve. Had the planet been cursed with his presence in those days, The Grand Religio-fucking-asshole-path would have been among the first to drill a worm into pissy Kryssie's emaciated love handles.

Are you aware of how much less imposing the Grand Religiopath looks when he's not sheathed in the sacred chasuble? There's a lot more to that vestment than spandex. Enough underwires to secure a concentration camp.

That's why I like it here amongst the Relic Amalekites: no religiopaths, no clergy/apparatchiks of any kind, and never have been since porno-scriptural times. Just a direct line to their particular dada in the sky, who seems less meddlesome than most, having written everything out beforehand and taken an especially long nap, or something. I'm not paying a whole lot of attention to that, and nobody expects me to.

Grand Religiopath unsheathed
in the sacred chasuble

Merely to harbor a phrase or two of this content on the premises would earn for our entire household the same horrific punitive sentence that Dad faces if he comes home for a birthday, or for any other reason.

Habit's a strong force. Here's what I hymn when pondering the passion of Krystelle Rex. As I go outside to exploit our single culinary resource, I sing, in the dead-ish liturgical lingo of our deoxyribonucleic faith—

Pluck forth thy coiffure's pathogens,
pluck forth thy locks entwined within,
pluck forth from radiant brows the flesh
which pads the seams where headbones mesh.

Pry back thy scalp like fecund sod,
expose thy rank farm's protein pods,
chip free thy skull, let marrow drain
till one grey tegument remains.

And when thy brain is amply shown,
and naught is left of skin and bone,
then serve thyself to KRYSTELLE REX,
or suffer our collective hex.

I've heard it's not unusual for estranged parents to employ offspring as both weapons and battleground. In our case the militarism is naturally exaggerated. The struggle takes on automatic religiose overtones, by virtue of our hereditary caste. Dad being exiled from, and we abiding in, this Sovereign Theocracy, the family romance becomes nothing less than micro-geopolitical. Mom's orthodox piety is engaged in a strategic battle with Dad's blasphemy.

My little sister and I will either snap in this tug-o'-war, or the prime contestants will mutually self-destroy. Our generation will be the only bits remaining on the battlefield, a doubly frayed bit of rope, looking like a two-headed serpent coiled, or maybe just tangled, on the dining room rug.

iv.

So, a trio of times daily, under the invisible supervision of Krystelle Rex, I mash down my coiffure so as not to look ridiculous, doff love-sarong and don dungarees for the same reason, and perform the immemorial chore of a cavalryman's eldest offspring. It's simplified because, like so many single parents, our Mom's menu is encompassed by a single dish. Bowl, rather.

At the foot of our meal table each morning, noon and night she stands, having laid aside the certified and registered battalion-issue splatter pic. Before we are permitted to lower spoons into our quasi-nutritious meal of one ingredient, Mom must proclaim words to this effect:

"All upper-mammaloids capable of choice should choose but one substance to subsist upon and ask for no more, in order to avoid differential pathogens. And, my youngsters, what is the second of the three reasons we maintain strict monophagy?"

the Designated Forager

Mom pauses for us to supply the response, which I never do, for my own civil-sacral safety. Sometimes Sissy, whose head is no longer capable of harboring a self-preservation instinct, manages to splutter out the required words via some neural phonetic memory-reflex:

"To postpone planetary depletion."

A duly baptized citizen would be forgiven for blushing and perhaps even diving out the dining room window at the sound of that phrase. Juxtaposing the words "planetary" and "depletion" is canonically prosecutable within the borders of a religio-political entity whose sole contribution to world culture is the most powerful biocide ever brewed.

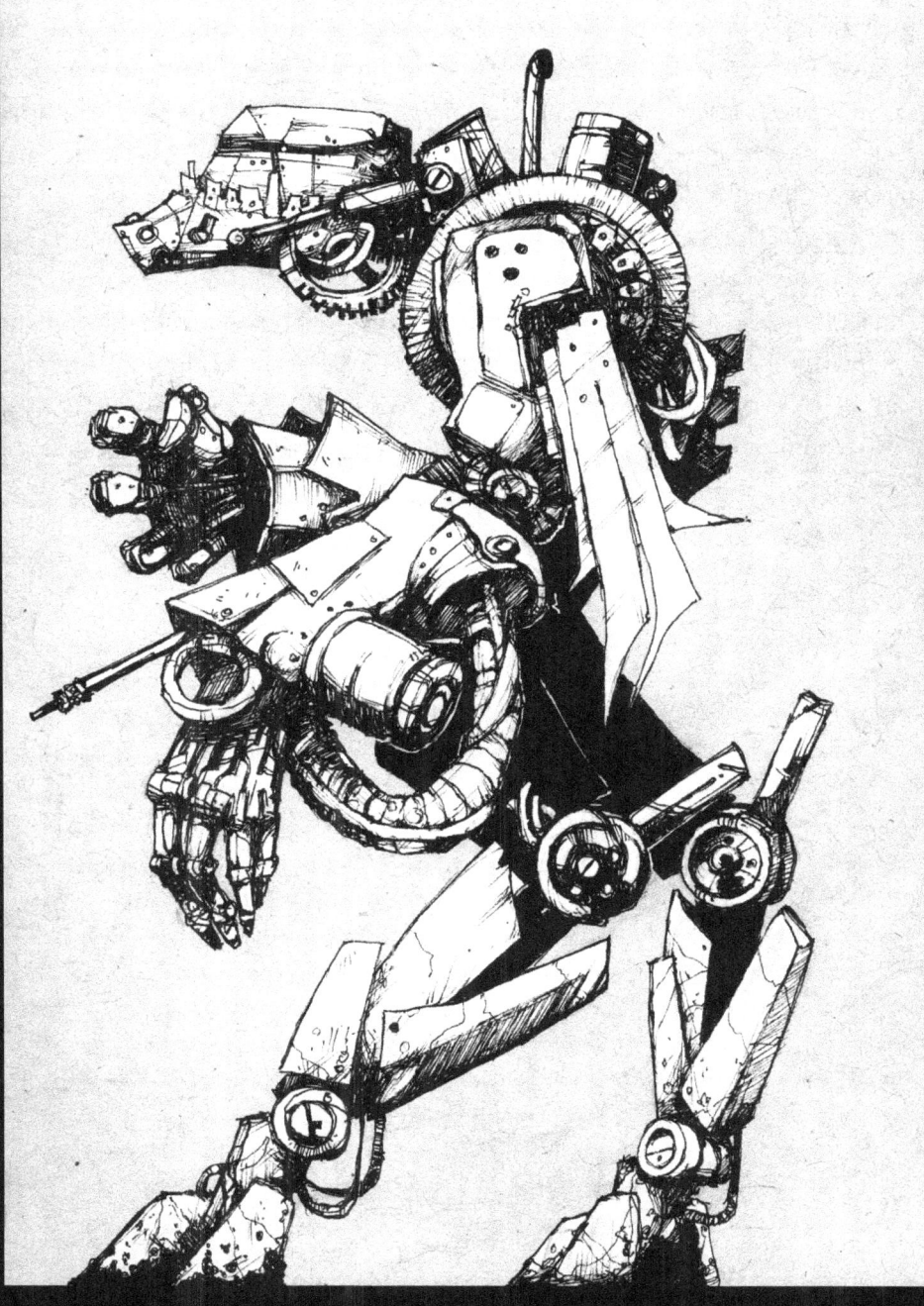

the expected civil servant

Fearless Mom continues her utterance in an even more perilous vein: "Yes, and just as importantly, we subsist monosubstantially to express solidarity with our Sovereign Theocracy's tragic victims on the trans-Judeuphrates bank."

Such dangerous talk would come as a surprise from any citizen of our Sovereign Theocracy. But it's particularly unexpected from someone who was ditched in those tragic trans-Judeuphratic victims' favor: the ex-wife of a traitor-infidel-defector-champion of lost causes who rides with the Relic Amalekites and has therefore been condemned in absentia to slow strangulation by means of his own intestines if he should ever set foot again in his homeland. (No wonder Dad misses all our birthdays.)

Can it be coincidental that her ex-husband happens to be frolicking through the foam of that dumped Flamma-Manna and galloping along the Middlingly Oriental wadis at the head of a Relic Amalekite cavalry regiment, under the banner of their officially debunked rival deity, whose blasted name I balk now to introduce to your ear?

What about the rind being bubbled
off their dear siblettes?

When she talks dirty like this, venting blasphemo-treason at the top of her lungs, Mom makes sure the dining room window's flung wide open to whoever or whatever might be eavesdropping in the backyard. It almost seems as though this naked woman hankers for a house call from the ever-expected civil servant who will handily put an end to our already twenty-five percent fragmented family romance once and for all.

She has caused it to be murmured around the riverside megalopolis that our household has adopted monophagia because she hears a "planetary cry of agony" each time our Sovereign Theocracy dumps a new batch of Flamma-Manna on our enemies.

"With each attack on the Middling Orient," she rants and shrieks as the three of us huddle around the four-seater meal table, "another potential food species is rendered extinct in the borderline-infertile home-sands of the long-suffering Relic Amalekites, and hence an ala carte item is erased from their ever dwindling menu. Is this just? Is this wholesome?"

"Menu curtailment, what an injustice!" I scoff, even though sarcasm works as well on Mom as sulphuric acid on glass. "What about the rind being bubbled off their dear siblettes?"

Little Sissy writhes empathetically. She vocalizes and strains against her feeding chair straps. I hate to exacerbate the miserable tenor of her existence, but I must emphasize my point, meanwhile watching and listening to her ever so carefully.

"We smite them and our poison settles down on the gummy sand to irritate their sweet little sissies' nasal passages and make them do the Sneeze Catastrophic. Just imagine that."

"Should we, then" continues Mom, ignoring my interruption and her younger child's tongue-swallowing seizure, "luxuriate in a multifarious diet replete with sauces and sorbets between courses? Monophagia can be the only fit expression of our national-racial-religious chagrin."

She fills our bowls with caps and stems of the Flyblown Fruiting Body, which has begun to grow in our backyard, perhaps not coincidentally, since the commencement of hostilities across the river.

V.

The debiologification of enemy land is happening so far away that you will be excused for not believing Mom's story about hearing agony-cries from such a distance—especially since she's lying.

Her nutritional monomania is indeed a response to hearing the plops of something being dropped on the "planetary epidermis." But it's an altogether different substance, and it's flopping down much closer to home.

Not unlike Flamma-Manna, this stuff's deposition is a direct result of the current state of worldly war. But it smells even worse than a military-industrial poison, and, in fact, it promotes the rankest vomiting forth of useful vegetation.

It's not being shat from machinery, but is rather extruded from the problematical rectums of creatures who have colonized our backyard. You could say the percussions of warfare have jostled these creatures to flock to the rear of our house, where they molt and roost. Or maybe I should say they shed and squat, for these roughly ambiguous avio-mammaloids are performing the second verb in more than one way. More squatters than roosters, in fact.

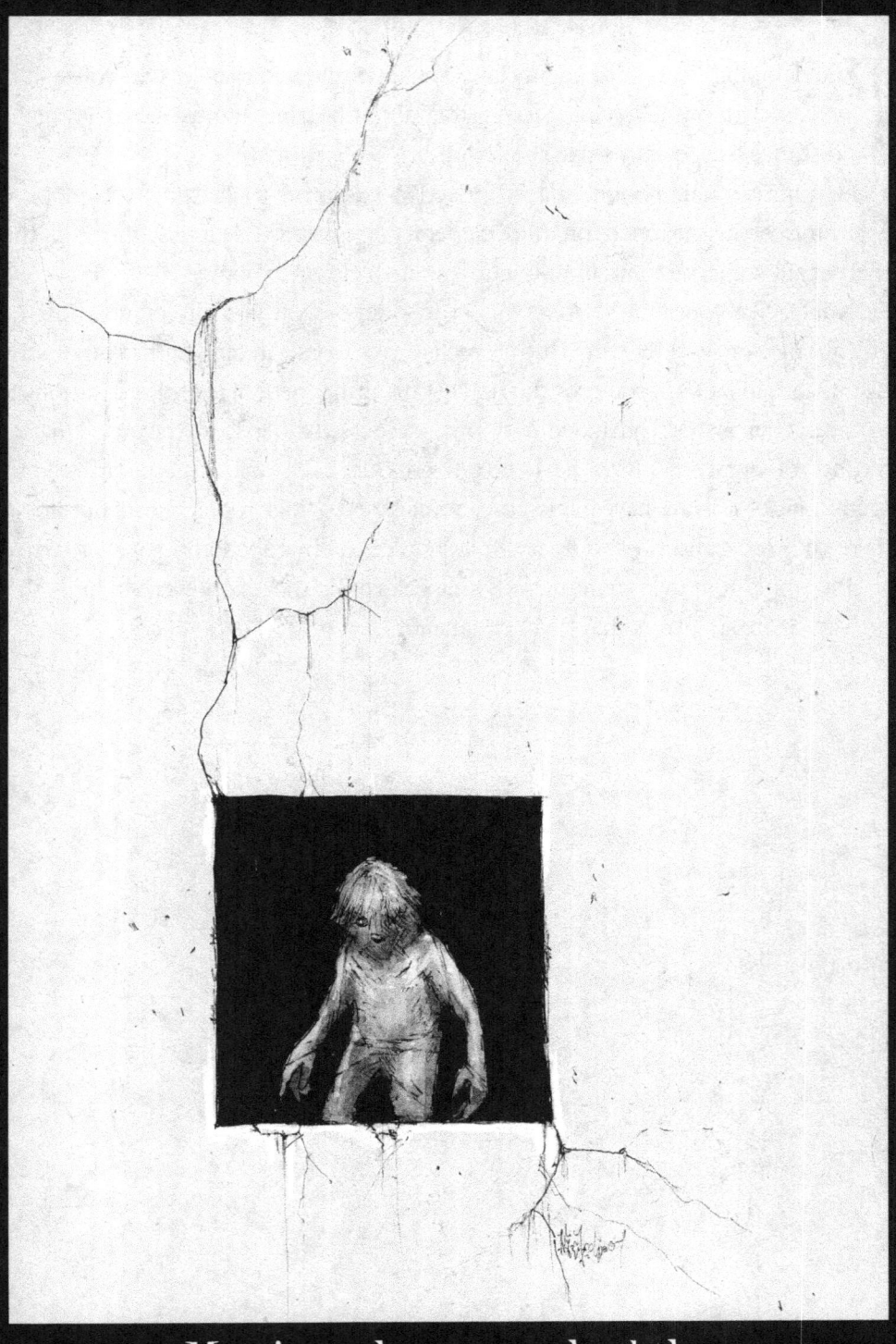

My sister has never had the
temerity to look out the window.

And, incidentally, they have, indeed, been hanging around our dining room window, eavesdropping and voyeuring, at least to the extent their bestial states of consciousness permit such sophisticated behaviors.

Meanwhile, these uninvited guests of ours generate an exploitable resource right under our dining room windowsill. Thus is promoted the monoculture of breakfast, lunch and supper (eucharist, too), to be conveniently and cost-effectively gatherable by the non-girl of the house, the foraging cavalryman's eldest spawn, the narrator of this family romance.

Sissy harbors certain elaborate and unshakeable delusions with regard to the physical appearance of the infesters and beshitters of the place where she used to play before losing her mind. She believes she can sense them peeking, listening and taking notes on Mom's blasphemo-treasonable shrieks, to be delivered into the claws of the same Grand Religiopath who long ago licked away my poor sissy's hymen as well as her capacity for sequential thought.

Sissy has certain inaccurate notions
about our squatters.

Sissy claims the ability to see, or at any rate to mentate our guests through the wallpaper and sheetrock and stucco. No doubt she's haunted by differentially configured demons who represent something unrelated, if no less horrible, in the deformed convolutions of her mind.

She has never had the temerity actually to look out and try to catch a glimpse, and she can't have actually seen their big plumage, bigger hands and arguable crotches. But however her destroyed mind's eye interprets their imaginary aspect, I don't doubt my sister apprehends our backyard campers' moral and spiritual reality with absolute clarity, like rat corpses phosphorescing among splintery joists.

I do realize and regret that my brief thrice-daily backyard sallies constitute desertion of this tiny lunatic. For no better reason than to stave off family starvation, I leave my siblette at the mercy of Mom's pathogens and other elaborate whims.

But Sissy would die of a brain seizure if she were even to consider following me out of Mom's eclipse, into the crawling, clamoring company of her outdoor terrors.

outdoor terrors

vi.

I t's only with reluctant effort that I recall a time when, like the young river-wading version of Dad, I too was up to my pube-line in warmish, gritty fluid. It's with amniosentimentality that I try to reestablish in my mind the mood of the moment when I was too young to be punished for maestrobation-qua-bedwetting in a pungent yet mollifying semen-urine blend, and could luxuriate awash in something resembling the Judeuphrates' poisoned saline solution.

I am speaking, of course, of having the ancestral faith imposed on me via the extraordinary expedient of intrauterine lavage, known in some quarters as amniobaptism. This is how, in our Sovereign Theocracy, the deterministic life-death sentence of caste is imposed.

Given the creepily implied Mom-proximity, it is with agonized reluctance and edge-ground teeth that I entertain such a dim memory of my ur-self, and assume this element to have been the filthy syrup styled, in some medical quarters, "amniotic." I must be reliving the prenatal trauma.

amniobaptism

It's as though my angle of vision is furnished through the meatus of one of those viddy-cams penised on the tip of a tubular endoscope stalk, and screwed into the maternal umbilicus in order to spelunk the ribbed mater-vault.

Karma, they say, is the mere handmaiden of heredity. I seem to have forded this figurative Judeuphrates before Dad blinked off the glint in his eye that produced me, before he absconded with the odd-toed ungulate to be a contractor or whatever among our nation/race/faith enemies.

And in my deja vulva I am fetal in some half-hatched way, so inexperienced as to smile at something, or someone, out of the frame which, or who, hasn't yet violated that smile, as they all eventually do. The river and sky are emblematic of Bitch Mother's innards, and there is neither backyard nor spying squatters to infest it.

Most survivors recollect as peaceful and comfy their spell awash in the endometriotic retch-sauce. You won't be surprised to hear that Bitch Mother spoiled that for me, in the name of pathogen-siccing. Already she was on the job, even before her poison broke.

our Sovereign Theocracy's shock-vergers

She inserted a pessary, and thereby dispatched an aborto-pathogen to swim after me, like one of our Sovereign Theocracy's shock-vergers chasing my Dad, trying to put an end to him before he can muck all the way across to the far bank and baste under the ostensible beneficence of the Middlingly Oriental rival god instead of Krystelle Rex.

This pessary was prescribed in a bolus by, of course, our Diocese-Certified Familopath and comic relief, crusty ol' Doc Clyster. It is the kind of aborto-virus that turns the peritoneal waterway bile-green with its approach.

But Mom only dispatched a semi-competent one. She did not want to procure good and proper miscarriage, just a half-incapacitated pup, like me, which is what she got. Somatically challenged, nipped in the bud. Easier to torment, presenting simple sado-challenges. She preemptively semi-unbegat me.

These things don't require a submerged environment to thrive. Gussied up and prettified as a purple flower bloom, they can follow you into existence and stalk you down the sidewalk with retro-abortifacient motives, like undercover priestcrafty assassins shadowing your dad through the Relic Amalekites' home-sand— especially if you have weakened your immune system with incessant maestrobation and have left yourself wide open to invasion by such pathogens as engender the Sneeze Catastrophic.

This, of course, is assuming I'm not the result of parthenogenesis. Or perhaps I appear now before your eyes via the expedient of pullulation. Was I reproduced asexually as a growth or warty excrescence on the mommish superficies, or maybe mashed amongst her innards, which became, at least superficially, a separate individual?

What if the person soon to be taken for "Dad" rode off immediately after meeting Mom? If he sneaked off with the odd-toed ungulate that was destined to be his true life companion before bothering to blastulate that month's Equestrienne Princess—and if Little Sissy is a trans-species facial-fornicatory bastardette, as Dad has always suspected—well, that begs the question of where the narrator of this family romance came from.

the kind of aborto-virus that
turns the river bile-green

vii.

Sissy knows her papa's true whereabouts, and they are cis-Judeuphratic, and she goes into conniptions if Mom or I try to suggest otherwise.

She has been in lust with the old man ever since coming close enough to his tickle-gizzard to be conceived by it (assuming she's not the bastardette he suspects her of being), and she refuses to believe Dad's a turncoat rider for the Relic Amalekites, or even an agent provocateur pricking flanks on behalf of the Divine Krystelle Rex (which is what I am sure crossed your mind already without my mentioning it). The only correct data her ruined consciousness has been able to assimilate regarding the current male-parental situation is that her beloved "papa" is gone, and that he abides among strange beings.

In going away to defy our condescending, paternalistic Sovereign Theocracy, Dad left a condescending, paternalistic void, which Sissy can only supply with denial and delusion. She can't accept that her father has been legally labeled such a monster that our own Grand Religiopath will personally execute him if he ever comes home for her birthday. So she projects the monstrosity instead upon a weak-chinned gaggle of backyard squatters.

bound in a bunker

She whispers to me, in terror, late at night, the news that her "papa" has been taken hostage by the guests whom she has visualized so horrifically and inaccurately. Dad has not really traversed a body of water, but has merely gone out of doors (which she is afraid to do) and is bound in a bunker sunken deep among the squatters' turds. He is going to be viddy-headed any minute, our Dad—rather, my poor siblette's papa.

"Want to know the saddest thing about it?" she used to weep, late at night when Mom appeared to be quasi-dormant, "Papa's handsome ride-loving buttocks haven't felt a saddle, but only the mud floor of a sub-excrement cell, the whole time he's been—" The pathetic child would shudder at her next word. "—outside!"

Of course, my half of our mutual dream-cloning of the father is influenced by his letters home, for I retain the ability to read. And, in any case, there is only a limited extent to which our shared paternal dreams can coincide, due to our almost opposite physical natures. I, being non-girlish, am expected to cherish a more-or-less heroic Dadotype, regardless of how it turns my stomach at times. Sissy, on the other hand, being unambiguously non-boyish, is saturated with Mommish-hormones, and therefore expresses her hallucinated anxiety for a Daddy that needs motherly cuddles, thus:

"Papa's a hostage in a backyard oubliette, posing for naked photos and taking neon tubes up the rectum! He is up to his powerful washboard waist in fluid, dungeon drainage, fellow decapitees' spinal sauce!"

Sissy's own spinal sauce is problematic enough.

She passes out completely when halluci-Dad looks up through the grating, smiles and says, "Just like me—

you're waiting to die

waiting

No wonder my little siblette is obdurate imagining our foreign guests as more horrible than ridiculous. She can have no idea how right she is about the, shall we say, earthy intimacy between Papa and, if not the squatters themselves, then certain of their further-off, less fortunate cousins.

viii.

Where did such a peculiar pair of siblings really come from? Do they necessarily share both parents? For all her protestations of pathogenophobia, it seems likely that Mom at least once allowed a certain differentially configured center of consciousness to mount her, to fasten onto her head, the Sneeze Catastrophic not only be damned, but courted, seduced.

I never saw her in her Equestrienne Princess morphosis, because she fleshed out immediately after I crawled like a worm-fish with newish leg sprouts from the mire inside her. But Dad insinuates in his letters that she formerly liked to sexualize more than the normally engaged organs and connective tissues, and to get herself blastulated by, shall we say, other than mainstream cooperators. Literate avians, for example. I wonder, and shudder, if that is where my own bookish bent originates, for I am a fan of the famous Diocesan Prize-Winning novelist/homilist, Blurt Vomitgut.

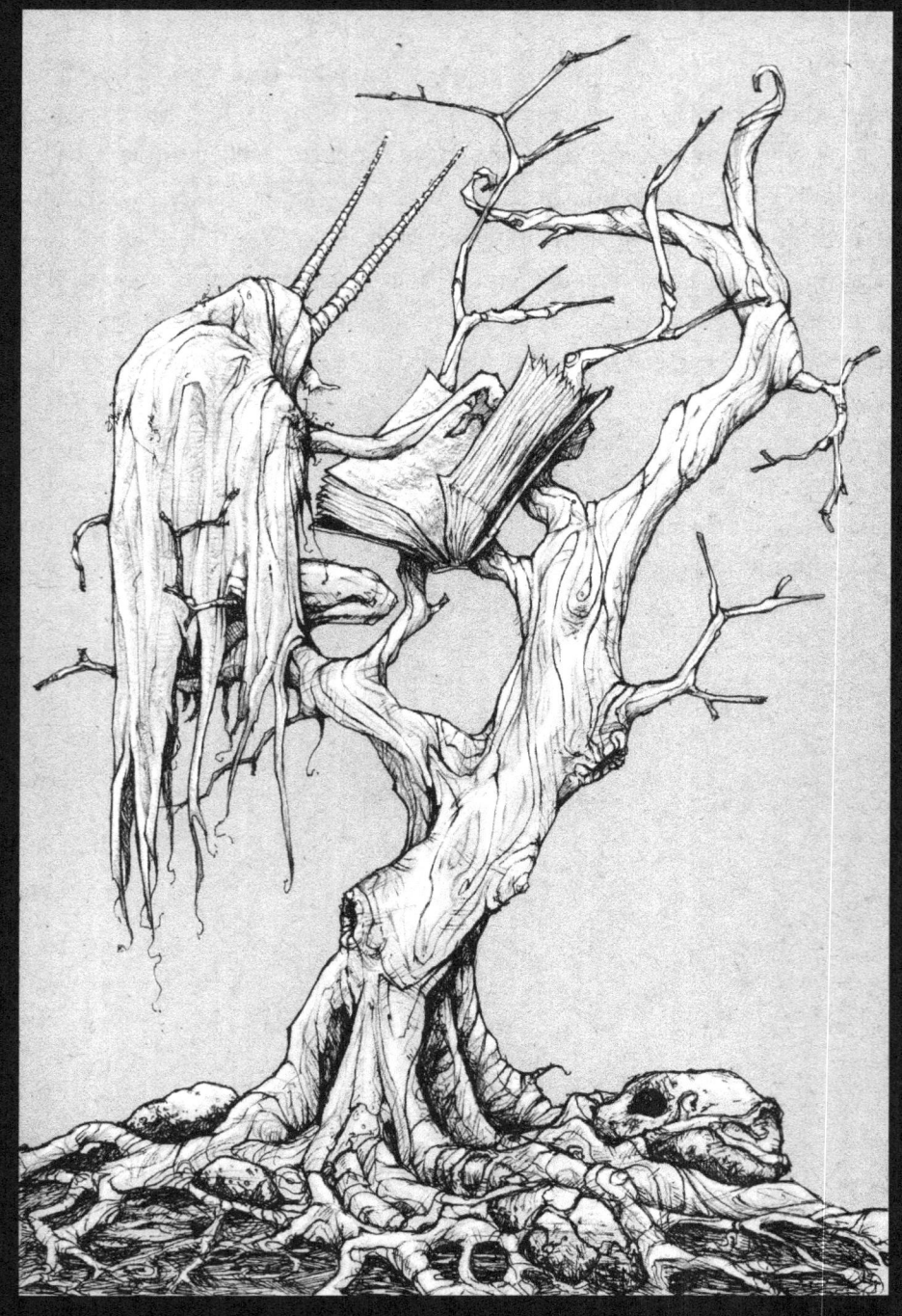

a certain differentially configured
center of consciousness that might be
Sissy's true Darwinistic papa

I believe this indiscriminateness is where the seeds, or maybe spoors, of her later pathogen anxiety were planted. She projects upon us not hypochondria so much as shame. In much the same manner an alternative fornicator will fret about T-cell count till he gives himself hydraulic apoplexy, his immune system meanwhile remaining pristine as the driven snow.

Dad was heard to speculate that Sissy might be the product of such a one-night facialization, "a loogy bastardette partial throat abort," as he quasi-spoonerized it.

Crusty ol' Doc Clyster, our Diocese-certified Familopath, is too professionally discreet to venture an opinion on the legitimacy of Daddy's ostensible seedlet, his little compulsive maestrobatrix. But the physician calculates that her original pre-civil/sacral strappado Intelligence Quotient was so emphatically through the roof "it must have been coated in avian excrement." I'll assume that's the sort of figure of speech employed by comic relief, and not a hint as to her biological father's species.

But no level of bastardy can adequately explain Sissy's present state of mind. Rather, mindlessness. So, what trauma caused her to doff her off-the-shoulder love-sarong and revert to pinafores and big-eyed mini-effigies and ghastly baby self-talk?

Sissy touches her dolly just like the
Grand Religiopath touched her.

I'm told it's the norm for immature mammaloids to gambol. But I can tell you the giggles emanating from pre-adult members of our Cavalry Caste are the most offputting noises outside a bonobo's asshole. Our playpen giggles sound like an emery board wiped against the whirling blades of a deep-fried toadstool shop's back alley exhaust fan. The sight of one of us skipping around the food table toting toys is emetic. We are Military down to our alleles, and meant to kill and explode things, not frisk and frolic. When one of us reverts to the youngster-sickness in adulthood, it could almost be considered a toxic medical waste disposal problem.

What trauma induced Sissy to revert? What caused her to shed so much of the high, elaborate, lovely coiffure Mom purchased for her head, all the better for unwellness vectors to perch and nest? Why did my siblette go for the top-knot and pigtail effect?

Blame for her state of, shall we say, "mind" is to be laid at the spandexed feet of the matched set of municipal priestcrafters who, with great officiousness, made a house call in tow of their horrendous boss, long ago, coincidentally around the time of the paternal defection.

If Dad had slipped too far away to be disemboweled and righteously throttled therewith, the Grand Religiopath and his assistants could gratify their holy urges by performing a not entirely dissimilar disservice to the soft tissues inside his younger offspring's pelvis and head, thus teaching the traitor-infidel's family a lesson.

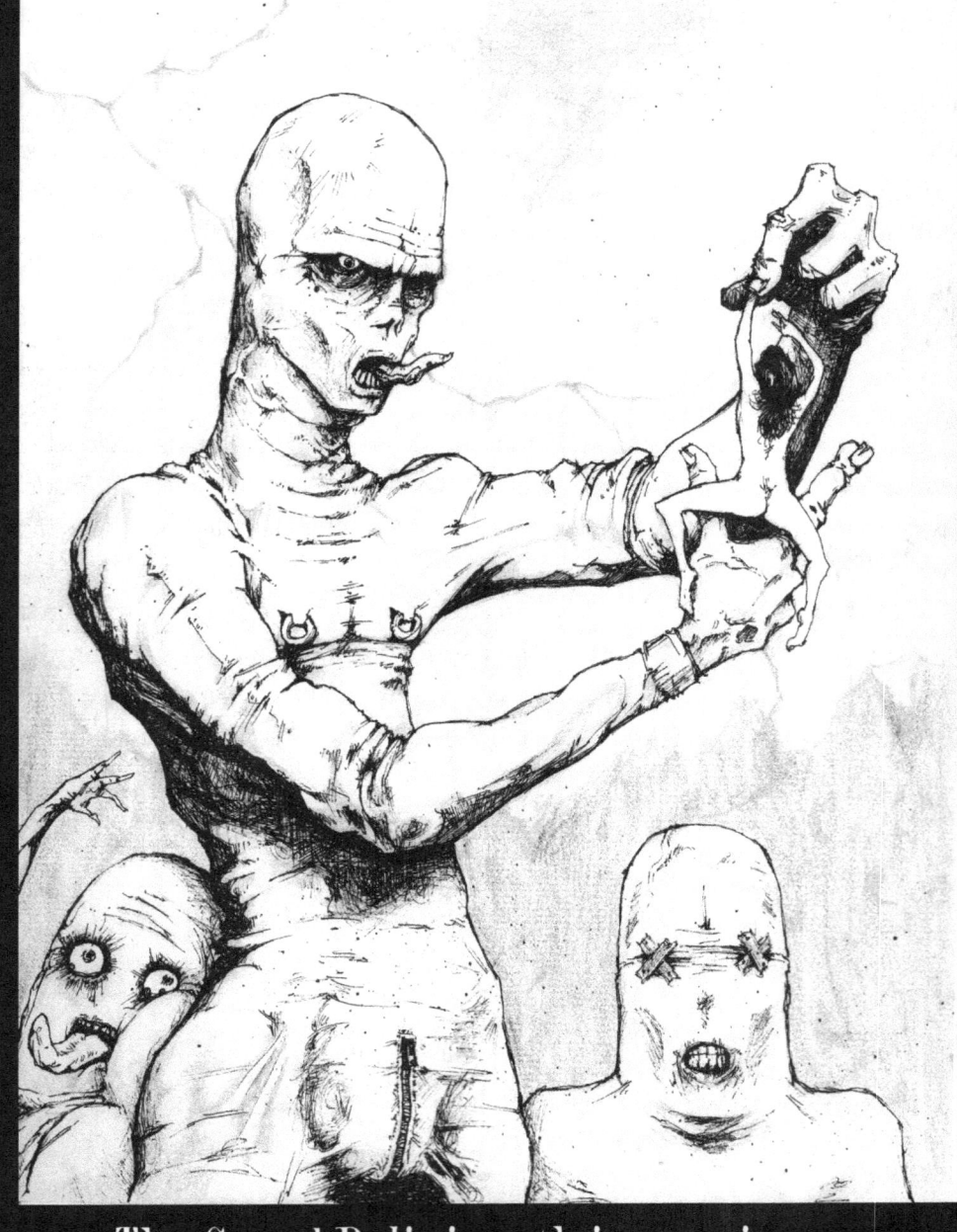

The Grand Religiopath improvises a
cunnilingual refinement on the
dread civil/sacral strappado.

So our domicile was graced with the presence of those distinguished types of personages who've abided in the seminary/barracks and have been decorated with the zippered codpiece and other sacerdotal paraphernalia. The Grand Religiopath and his peers generally prefer inquiring into the more frankly penised youth of the faith. But in Sissy's case they made an exception, and consented to accept her as a catechumen and bless her.

The Grand Religiopath was supplicated to perform an intrusive yet exploratory inquisition into my little sister's nether-soul, in search of elementary spirits that wanted casting out, or "exvaginated," to use the canonically approved Latinism. They tried her via the dread civil/sacral strappado with a cunnilingual refinement, an innovation specially extemporized on the spot by the Grand Religiopath himself, a rare honor.

They wrung Dad's only daughter dry of self-possession, then left her dribbling and spasming in the worst possible custodial care: namely, Mom, who makes the entire national clergy look like rank lay-civilian hobbyists in the brain-reaming department.

He tried the refined civil/sacral
strappado on Mom — once.

ix.

Therefore, I do feel terrible leaving the child alone in the dining room with our tormentor thrice daily. But mine is a temporary siblette abandonment, and necessary to our physical survival—in more ways than one.

one familistic type metabolizing another

Aside from supplying boluses and chymes for the perpetuation of our respective peristalses, my forays serve an emotional purpose: a release of red steam, a postponement the sort of love explosion that ends with one familistic type metabolizing another, leaving little more than shrapnels of connective tissue on the dining room rug like vaguely decipherable red runes. This romance in your hands may very well end with something scribbled and stomped.

Such a horrendous climax to this family romance could be put off indefinitely, or at least postponed till it wouldn't appear premature, if I only had an emotional outlet. Say, an affectionate pet to commiserate with, to whom I could condescend without sarcasm, whose mind hasn't been poisoned against me.

During the relatively halcyon years before worldly war brought foreign squatters flocking into the backyard, we begged Mom long and hard for a lower being of one configuration or another to love under the dining room window (hoping against hope that, if she agreed, she wouldn't immediately faciate with it and blastulate us a sibling with envenomed gills or something).

"Mom," Sissy whined (this was before she surrendered most of her rational capacity and tongue flexibility to the priestcrafters), "a lovely pet might suck into its own sinuses a few of the pathogens that are so intent on catastrophically sneezing the vitality out of us."

Mom just sneered in reply. "Youngsters," she hissed. "should be content to have their faces licked and their thighs dry-humped by the vermin that already come with the house."

But then the squatters came flocking to our backyard, those ambiguous avio-mammaloids who fill my sister's head with such horrible, if completely inaccurate, images of themselves. Their arrival forcedour loving parent to reconsider her decision regarding a guard pet.

Mom only let us have
pretend backyard animals,

Was it in order to alleviate her daughter's horror of these delusion-exacerbated bugaboos that Mom decided to procure a more or less bestial deterrent for their approach to our dining room window? What do you think? Mom had personal reasons for changing her mind. And they were less motherly than geopolitical, less geopolitical than hygienic.

She'll protest dietary solidarity with them before each meal. She'll restrict her offspring to an almost lethally jejune diet on their behalf. But Mom's too pathogen-minded to sit still while they pile their shit hip-deep behind our house.

Yes, perhaps you will not be surprised to hear that the squatters happen to be none other than Relic Amalekites. These are the very wretches on behalf of whose stuck-at-home cousins we've become monophages, whose cries of Flamma-Manna agony Mom claims telepathically to hear, all the way from the trans-Judeuphrates.

Our municipal zone has experienced an influx of these Middlingly Oriental war refugeniks. Our holy colonialism, our religio-imperialism, our doctrine of Conversion by Defoliant has come home to roost and molt. And squat and shit.

the kind of vermin that
already come with the house

They feel free hobo-jungling on our property because of what they presume to be our politics. But, little do they know, the missing man of this house harbors motives of his own for taking part in the hopeless resistance against the biocide and occupation of their home-sand. And it's not in the name of their liberation that Dad has given himself whole-body terminal saddle sores.

whole-body saddle-sores

It turns out Sissy was righter than she could have known about them. In her paranoia she accurately surmised their ethnicity/species, probably before you did. But their politics are a matter of indifference to her. All she knows is that Papa is gone, and the Grand Religiopath cunni-strappadoed her for it, and bogeys are holding her papa in a backyard bunker under a pile of excessive turds.

surgical Flamma-Manna on-the-ground applicator for those hard-to-reach nooks of biology

Still gritty behind the ears (assuming they grow ears), these refugeniks, autochthonous and immemorial natives of the Middling Orient, are heli-dumped into our laps as ever larger quadrants of their tragically war-torn region are rendered uninhabitable and subsequently occupied.

How does the Grand Religiopath persuade our youngsters to put on boots, fix bayonets on their Diocese-issue pistols and wade across to sizzle and blister on Flamma-Mannaed turf—rather, sand—which is so poisonous that its sting can be felt through neoprene? Well, let's just say (speaking frankly) that the occupation of the trans-Judeuphrates is not exactly being carried out by our Sovereign Theocracy's most intelligent subjects.

not our most intelligent subjects

In a secret letter home, Dad has supplied further elucidation of the situation—

In a disingenuous display of faux-group guilt, our—rather, your—Sovereign Theocracy welcomes a tiny trickle of these wretches in without bothering them to master the local lingo, nor asking them to modify their quaint native rind. Witness, for example, their offputting shoulder dentition, and so forth. The obvious ulterior motive of such noblesse oblige is the conversion of these infidels to the One True Faith in your mother's slavering masochistic Kryssie-pootums. Good Luck.

The Relic Amalekites themselves, valuing their timeless heritage less than I do, want nothing to do with biocidal agents, and even less with idiot foreign foot soldiers. One might almost guess they'd grown tired of the desert long before this, judging from the eagerness with which they come to you in search of a better way of life—which, from the sound of it, comprises the steadfast production of bowel movements in citizens' backyards.

squatters in more than one sense

family / romance

I hesitate to offend political sensibilities, if any remain in this time of worldly war. But it becomes necessary at this point to discuss certain aspects of their personal hygiene, as they pertain to the very survival of the family that modifies this romance, and in particular to Mom's acquiescence to our weeping pleas for a pet.

Having been nomads since the dawn of sentient history, and having enjoyed till recently a broad range upon which to deposit their turds, our foreign friends are like bonobos who, despite relatively large cephalic indices, must never be allowed to go undiapered in a domesticated context because, in the wild, all they had to do was hang their elaborate nether-vents off the residential bough and swirl out bogs. Our backyard squatters can never be persuaded to leave their turds in a single circumscribed quadrant of the backyard—an advanced bit of calculus which even the average cyno-pet has no difficulty mastering. It would make my foraging chore easier, if not less unappetizing.

Tiptoeing has become the rule of the day for me as I gather our familistic calories from amongst the alien feculence. And, as if to endorse the Darwino-heresy, our visiting fecundators themselves seem adapted peculiarly well for tiptoeing, as they lurch about on downright struthious gams.

With such legs, feathers and talons, it's no wonder they got along so well with the first pet we persuaded Mom to get us.

X.

Here's a notion of how deep Mom's politicization flows. For her, the outbreak of worldly war and geno-biocide necessitated nothing more or less drastic than the purchasing and posting of an attack animal to stem the localized shit-flow.

So she acquiesced, and got us the sort of pet that comes recommended for a fundamental social unit of our socioeconomic level—namely non-mammaloid. Her only stipulation was that it should possess beak and talons sufficiently pugnacious to discourage the approaches of foreign anuses to our dining room window.

Like its cousins the sparrows, who camp-follow and settle on odd-toed ungulate droppings behind mobilized cavalry units the world over, our first pet (her name was Winfrey) fed off shit. It was only natural behavior, and to be expected. The creature failed to keep the spies from our dining room window, of course, as they were living snack machines.

if only I had an affectionate pet,
named Winfrey, to love...

In fact, the Relic Amalekites suborned Winfrey with their fragrant productions—but not the nutritious fungus that sprang therefrom. Those Winfrey beaked fastidiously forth, coated with bilious saliva till unpalatable to any self-respecting upper-mammaloid, and spat out to rot in the grass.

So not only did that bird-brain fail to protect our privacy, but she deprived us of our sole source of calories—for we are myco- as well as monophages. Our bio-caste feeds exclusively off fungus sprung from feces. Did I forget to mention that? Our meals consist of spoor-bearing bodies tumored from refugeniks' backyard bowel movements, specifically the stems and caps of the Flyblown Fruiting Body. The intestinal congestion expelled throughout our backyard by our foreign guests turns out to be the ideal incubator, almost as lush and fecund as agar-agar in a petri dish.

And what crawls with more pathogens than the former contents of beastly bowels? You begin to see how inspired is Mom's choice of emotional control mechanisms. Shall I begin to enumerate the bushel-baskets of fecal fungus Bitch Mother urges us to eat? Between the two of us, my tiny, frail, emaciated siblette and I consume more spoor-bearers per day than flourish in a year on the Augean floor of a poorly janitored bovine diarrhea ward.

Sometimes I wonder what our dad would say if he knew this about the refugeniks whose home-sand he is trying so unpatriotically and sacrilegiously (if perhaps a tad sarcastically) to liberate: if ever repatriated through his efforts, they would deprive his estranged family of caloric intake. Talk about a conflict of interest—assuming Dad's interested enough in us to be conflicted.

xi.

Mom was sold on religiosity as a parenting tool when Siblette ran afoul of the Grand Religiopath. We couldn't help but notice how thoroughly he and his pair of priestcrafter-sidekicks ream-jobbed the poor child's rational capacity.

When the outbreak of fresh (if that's the word) hostilities between us and the Relic Amalekites spirited Mom's hubby away from her affections and alienated his loyalty from her Sovereign Theocracy, Mom decided that prayerific overtones should be morbidly forced upon all food and other oral intakes until such time as her favorite unambiguously male propinquity's triumphal return, even if it be in a zipper-bag.

Plus, all the mumbo-jumbo over the table had the added advantage of making her appear, to any ostensible dining room window peekers, to be a single mother seeking solace for her pitiful semi-orphans in religification: a real figure of pathos, as perceived by Relic Amalekite organs of discernment.

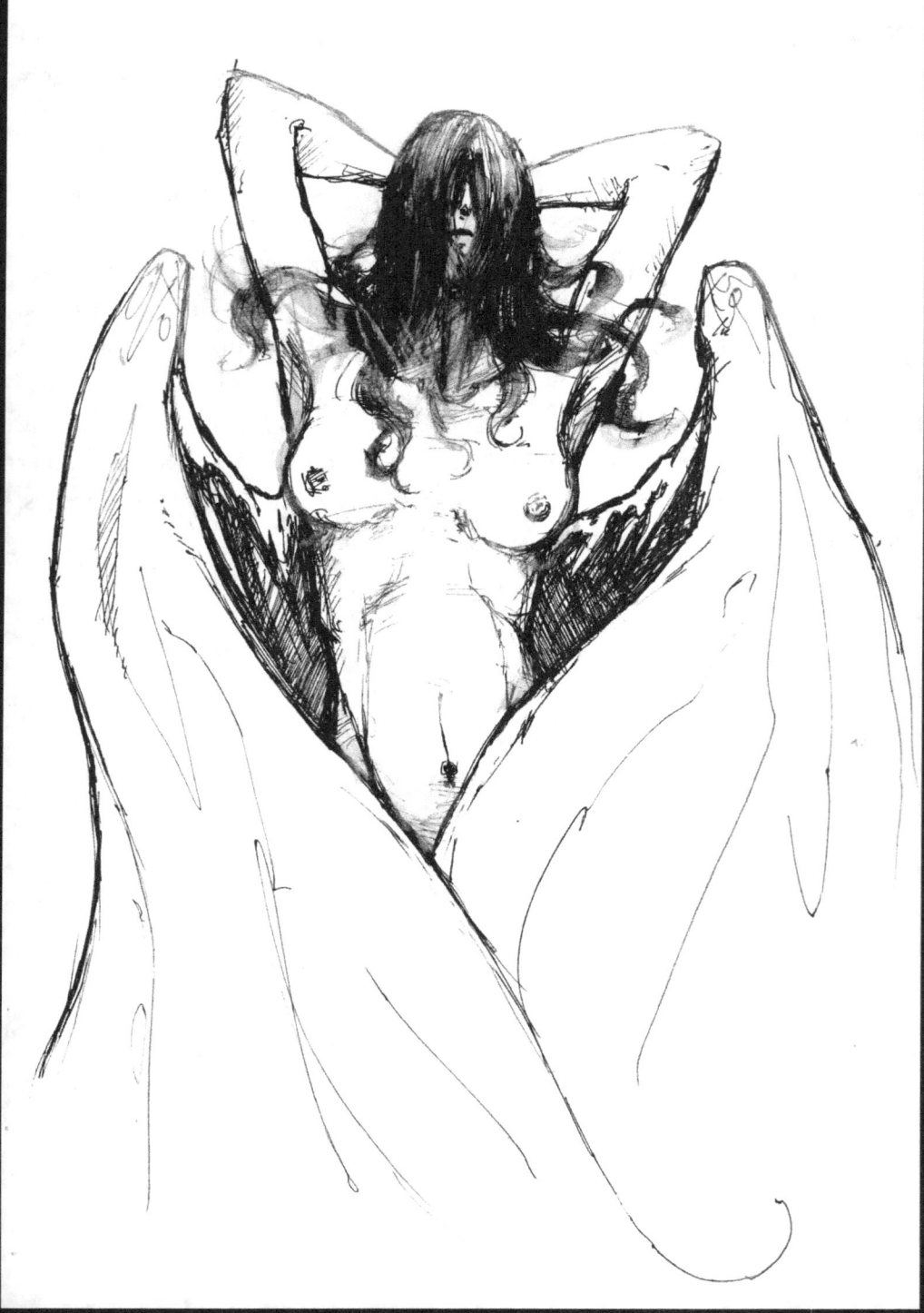

Mom's mumbo-jumbo at the table

When her husband mobilized off in brazen defiance of our Sovereign Theocracy and the state-priestcraft for which it stands, that's when Mom decided to go all mycosophical on us. Of course, it was a great coincidental help that we were already monophagous mycophiles.

Being a natural economizer, like so many un-double parents, she decided to go the indigenous route, to save on props and costumes. She furtively mailed away for shamaness certification, because, liturgically, it requires little more than nudity.

Thus she spared herself the expense of the pricey spandex gear of the board-certified priesthood of our proper federal faith. In any case she considers their zippered codpieces not only tasteless, but implicitly sexist in their gender-specificity. Besides, how can a minister primp and preen so, in spite of the pube-up nakedness Krystelle Rex displays in all iconic representations? Nudity is more congruent.

So here you have the true irony—no, absurdity—behind the Relic Amalekites being heli-shat into our particular backyard with the ulterior motive of their proselytization. Their house mother forsook the orthodox ways of Krystelle Rex long ago to profess Mycosophy, a faith even more divergent from our state norm than the Relic Amalekites' own monotheism.

Nudity is more congruent for Mom.

Having passed the novitiate in the mail-order myco-seminary, Mom is obliged to consider all meals, indeed, all ingestions, sacramental. And she encourages between-devotional snacks.

Handfuls of non-sentient life forms that can be found in the backyard do the sacramental trick. There is no outlay for postage on eucharist wafers, because turd-'shrooms are the official holy food of her particular denomination. I guess you could call it transcultural symbiosis.

You've met the types, the ones who build an entire existence around 'shrooms. That, I fear, is us. This is a myco-mush subsisting family. Citing starving Relic Amalekites (not the ones at the window, but their cousins across the river—who have more immediate concerns than peckishness, such as their bones emerging in the white phosphorus glow of Flamma-Manna), Bitch Mother makes poor, problematically nourished Siblette and me eat our fungus beyond the point of it coming out our ears.

Not only Sissy, but even I hallucinate little naked men and women sprouting spontaneously from the Flyblown Fruiting Bodies. Mom calls them, too, "pathogens," of course, and reminds us that each mealtime is yet another reason to cover our faces with both hands when we feel a Sneeze Catastrophic coming on.

Winfrey spits out the good bits.

As for the flavor, well, Mom says, "It is solely in order to postpone malnutrition that we swallow much of the material which gets deposited in our oral cavities from time to time. Food is not for titillating the senses."

It's almost suppertime. Hear Mom hissing from the food prep nook:

"Wash u-u-u-u-u-up!"

So, when Winfrey began scarfing up the fertilizing agent for our breakfast, lunch, dinner and, yes, eucharist, and potential caloric intake began to disappear from my foraging grounds, and our stomachs began to growl, Mom called the priestcrafters to put our idiotically failed guard pet down.

The Grand Religiopath, who is no mycophage, came within a feather of a free poultry meal. He prefers to eat things live, slowly tongue-rasping them away, atom by atom, to prolong the agony and damnation. Sissy went comatose in anticipation of his house call.

Mom salvaged a fashionable boa from Winfrey's remains.

Fortunately for Winfrey, before the Grand Religiopath could find time to drop by, a classic Mom pathogen mounted her head, precisely because she'd been ignoring Mom's warnings about eating feces like some brutish sparrow. The poor beast wound up sneezing all her soft bodily tissues away in aerosol form.

Sissy learned a lesson or two in virtuosic nasal bulemia pondering Winfrey's remains—out of which Mom improvised a feather boa. Pietistical hypocrite and vicious soul glutton though she be, Mom does have a certain fashion sense, for someone who dresses cheaply.

xii.

Mealtimes have a strange effect on my thoughts.

If you could have seen how Mom behaved at the memorial meal we improvised for Winfrey, you would understand why she wants no eyes or ears peeking and listening in on our family romance.

Perhaps it's the hyper-religiose overtones Mom slathers over them like some cloying giblet gravy, but even non-funereal mealtimes at our house take a strange effect on my thoughts and the inner pictures that accompany, or perhaps spur them.

In trying to steer through this maternal cyclone, I have had a rudder and compass. Under Dads' letters' influence, I've turned to literature. Deprived of an outlet for my fundamentally unwholesome urges, I discovered reading instead, and came to know the books of the more or less almost great-ish—

Blurt Vomitgut

—which were written deliberately on an infantile comprehension level in these days of childish literacy, thus depriving the author of full-grown adult self-expression, thus circumventing any writer's only reason for birth, thus leading inevitably to suicide attempts. This self-sacrifice on behalf of Blurt Vomitgut's base fans moved my Dad, who is tinctured deep in self-expungatory urges, like all full-blooded Military Casters.

Blurt Vomitgut's pot boilers are blabbed and regurgitated in rapid succession, one after another, if not simultaneously.

Dad recommended Blurt Vomitgut to me as a Mom antidote and role model: "If your fingers are full of inked styli, you must drop that tickle-gizzard for a season or so. Plus, the Blurt-man has a thing or two to say about mothers, having been nightmarishly mothered himself in times gone by."

Here's Mr. Vomitgut on that sore subject:

Orally gratifying religiosity, eucharistic pietism—the whole hyped-up scam of theophagy appeals to these so-called motherly types because it affords another, literal way for them to force their diseased will beyond our sinuses and extremities and directly, materially down into our guts. It's all we can do to roll our eyes broadly enough to make them self-conscious, to dissuade them from saying, "Take, eat, this is my body," as they sling those sacramental trenchers.

Blurt Vomitgut

Uncanny, right? It's almost as if Mr. Vomitgut is describing my own situation.

Our remaining parent's nothing if not possessed of a highly developed sense of impropriety. In her liturgical mode, such as she affects at those family dysfunctions called funerals, Mom flits and flaps around labially. She suits up like a regular ordained vestal of the Grand Religiopath himself, and grabs the Ancestral Riding Crop in both hands.

At such times her torso assumes such a certifiably erotic air, it's almost possible to ignore the giant hump that erupts from the dorsal area of all more or less healthy Cavalry Caste females when in thanato-estrus.

Unlike certain other nation-races, our citizenship passes with indifference, agnatic or matrilineal. And you can tell my mom is full-blood cavalry, eldest spawn to boot, by the way her parent rides posthumously on her back. This accords with the bio-mytho-ethic of our caste: the Cavalryman saddles up as a youth, dismounts at maturity, and remounts after death upon the eldest spawn, in the form of a doubly prehensile hump of greater or lesser substantiality, a semi-incarnation, only intermittently material, depending on hormonal and/or geopolitical circumstances. Mom must have been the eldest seed, because, from sacroiliac to nape, she bears this auric embodiment of the paternal nature, like a somatic patronym.

It's almost possible to ignore her
doubly prehensile hump.

family / romance

It's a semi-metensomatotic piggyback ride, cavalry-style, which is unlikely to skip the present generation. And my dread is that she will try to wrap her thighs around my shoulders some day, before the time is ripe, when those thighs still course with the blood that makes her so pathological, before that red gravy has had a chance to sublimate into the quintessence of spirit. Like the odd-toed ungulates we all are under the skin, she might jump the gun in this terminal derby. Then who will be the warty outgrowth on the superficies of whom?

We spend our lives mounted, and our deaths being mounted—unless we slip into decadence, like half of the current house- and backyard-bound generation, regressively bred to complete ineffectuality.

Sissy would lose control of bladder and bowels if ever brought into the presence of an odd-toed ungulate, or even an even-toed one. And I intend never to travel beyond our backyard, and to struggle with no enemy more formidable than refugeniks.

My dread is that Mom will jump the gun.

xiii.

As these are not the sorts of secrets Mom would want foreign savages voyeuring through the dining room window, she consented to the procurement of a proper attack mammaloid, once we'd scraped most of Winfrey's shit-fed atoms off the wallpaper. When we redeemed this secondary creature from the Diocesan Pound, it seemed to come fully equipped, with teeth and fur and everything, along with—or so I hoped—the mammaloid's capacity for at least aping the outward grimaces and twitches of affection. We named the weird bitch Hildegarde von Bingo and posted her in the backyard.

It is strange that Mom worried about our particular voyeurs, to the extent of kicking loose funds for a second pet. It's not as though the Relic Amalekites could spread rumors among minds capable of forming bad, or even good, opinions about us. Indiscretion presupposes the ability to transfer intelligibility, and these are foreigners, after all. They can't even talk, not in the proper sense of the term. Let's just say, for now, that the Relic Amalekites rely on nonverbal communication skills.

On the other hand, if Sissy is to be believed, they—or, rather, her distorted version of them (unfeathered, more terrible than ridiculous)—do make some kind of noises with their upper respiratory tracts. Like Mom pretending to hear the long-distance shrieks of their stay-at-home cousins as the skin melts off their skeletons in lumpy streams of Flamma-Manna, Sissy auditorially hallucinates our squatters' bestial vocalizations in the backyard.

As if deliberately to exacerbate Sissy's imagined agony with a stab of actuality, these savages have adopted the dining room window as their favorite place of social resort. Just exactly as before on Winfrey's watch, they like to hover and amuse themselves by observing our family romance unfold as Mom rapes her two whelps of self.

Meanwhile they play fetch with Winfrey's replacement, the very cyno-pet that is supposed to be barking them off. Hildegarde von Bingo was purchased to lick my face and dry-hump my thigh, not the homologous segments of their heads and legs. Loyalty to purchaser is one of the chief traits touted in the promotional material for this species of lower mammaloid, but only till the warranty dries up and crusts over, which it must have already done. Hildegarde von Bingo loves the intruders more than she does me.

Sissy can hear her distorted versions of them.

They have managed to suborn our second familistic pet as handily as they did the first, poisoning her mind against me every bit as thoroughly as they did Winfrey's. But this time, for a change, the thirty pieces of silver did not fall out of their assholes. It's not with the usual oral gratification the refugeniks have managed to purchase our guard-mammaloid's loyalties. Fecal snacks have not entered into the process of corruption, Hildegarde von Bingo being, anomalously enough for her kind, indisposed to shit eating.

Rather, the trick has been turned by cajolery of a sort that can almost be called borderline-linguistic, conveyed by what can only be called visual cues, for they tend to communicate by retina rather than auditory nerve. Their tongues being in their fingers, so to speak, the Relic Amalekites' quasi-language is uttered silently, by sign rather than phoneme—that is, if you are willing to call flipping the bird ninety-seven different ways chit-chat.

Paradoxically, this should be the one means of communication unavailable to a creature which suffers Hildegarde von Bingo's particular handicap. The miserable cur could not be less suited to respond to hand yammer and other sorts of visual clues. She's been rendered eyeless as her new masters are tongueless. Samson hitting rock bottom in the Gaza Strip was no less myopic than our mammaloid.

Pathogens such as this are not the culprits bringing blindness to our backyard mammaloid.

This particular rapine is not Mom's doing, for a change. Pathogens have not caused Hildegarde von Bingo to sneeze her eyes out. Nor is it the sacred handiwork of the priestcrafters reaming her optic nerves the same way they reamed Sissy's brain. Look toward our family wellness bringer, instead: crusty ol' Doc Clyster.

XIV.

A Like all responsible citizens, we intended to spay our pet upon its redemption from the Diocesan Pound when, avian love having failed, a mammaloid seemed to be indicated, instead, to guard our dining room window: the fur- and tooth- bearing type that needs neutering. But we made the mistake of hiring our Bishopric Approved Familopath to proceed with the intrusion, namely—

crusty ol' Doc Clyster

Like many comic reliefs, he's ill-at-ease around wholesome beings. Hence his choice of professions and his willingness to spend time in our presence. They say his deep education in bodily things has opened up a part of his brain that is closed in most, giving him access to rare wisdom, which, of course, has sickened him because he knows things far too disgusting for us mere lay-ignoramuses to imagine. That's why people are willing to pay him so much money to keep his mouth shut, pouted under immobile flounder-folds of pudge.

His abstruse knowledge is rumored to have cracked apart a window frame that is painted shut in most heads, a jagged aperture that opens into the secrets of the Family Romance. Of course, this wisdom has nauseated crusty ol' Doc Clyster on a terminal basis, and has caused his face to puff up in a permanent sneer of revulsion.

He's got the Hippopleptic Oath tattooed on the very ventricles of his gore pump, except for the line about those pessary-thingies that get poked inside moms—otherwise he would have attracted no patronage from our household in the first place. He only made that exception in Bitch Mother's case because he likes going up inside her on a clinical basis. "It's an education in itself," he assures me, with an upper-middle wink.

Of course, contact buzz from the Flyblown Fruiting Bodily potency stored in Mom's endometrio-sacs is what opened the peep-hole amongst Doc's forehead pleats. Some attach high spiritual significance to the eyeball that seems to have wedged itself in that hole. I suspect it's just a zit into which a pathogen with an eye spot has decided to hibernate.

They say his pseudo-third eye spot enables him to effect miracles, such as commanding respect from society, even though he spends all day elbow-deep in other people's mucous membranes. His right hand smells so bad it glows and stings the eyeballs, yet we must grovel at his three-toe slippers and salivate him "sensei" in the Nippo-manner. It's not fair.

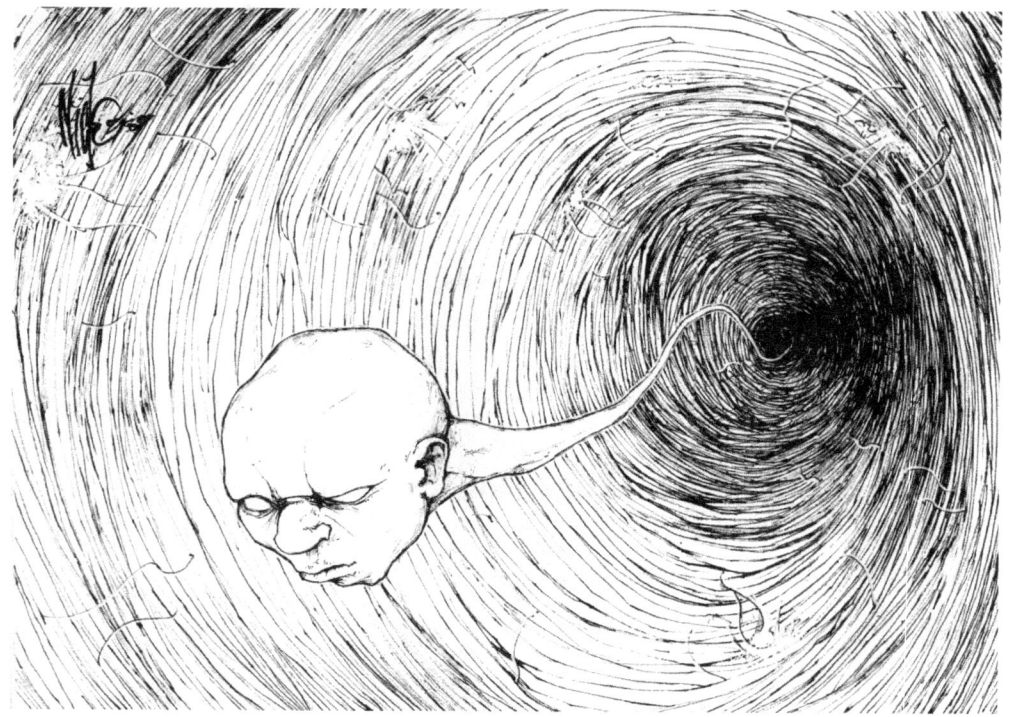

He likes going up inside Mom on a clinical basis.

As it turns out, ol' Doc Clyster is either hard of hearing or just possessed of an exceptionally chaste mind. In either case, with regard to our newly acquired attack pet, the only word he heard Mom say was "balls," and he went after the pair above the waist. He scooped out the windows of Hildegard of Bingo's soul rather than the sumps of her libido.

So, three times per day I must make a few judicious throat-clearings as I sphincter myself through the dining room window, to forewarn Hildegard of my approach before I come to ground behind our house, where, in swirls of black mist, the unfaithful beast has been chained.

Before setting to work, I take a brief moment and attempt mutually to commiserate with her. But she mocks my advances and condescends to me instead of vice-versa.

How the accursed refugeniks managed to bring about this unnatural state of affairs was a mystery at first. Even if she weren't unsighted it wouldn't have been easy. To measure the difficulties our foreign squatters would meet trying to make sweet talk to a mammaloid, or to any other sentient being, I invite you simply to observe them idly passing the time in our backyard.

Our backyard mammaloid, Hildegard von Bingo, is taught to signify just like a Talibanger.

Try to see them as they really are, unfiltered through Sissy's schizoid corneas, and you will notice that, in posture and gesture, they bear an uncanny resemblance to our own homegrown melano-youth gangsters who breed in the dioxin sludge of our Sovereign Theocracy's blight: those halitotic Gang-Talibangers who loiter and

halitotic Gang-Talibanger, disaffected,
ethno-bred in the dioxin-sludge linoleum of
the riverside megalopolis' melano-blight mall

smack and finger-signify along the superficies of disaffected idleness, who, in their fundamental perversion, sport their love sarongs on the only place Krystelle Rex didn't wear his.

The first few times I faced our displaced intruders and tiptoed among their, shall we say, self-evidence, I wondered who corrupted these poor war victims. Who taught them to sign as glibly as any machine-pistol-packing rapist who creeps along the pastel bubblegummy linoleum in one of the riverside megalopolis' metro malls? In outrage, I rhetorically demanded of Krystelle Rex to know who schooled them in the self-conscious posturing of the arms at lowland gorilla angles, in what might be called an act of kinesthetic reversion. Who persuaded the Relic Amalekites to "talk" with the same sort of sinister paw gyrations which criminals utilize to work out their sordid schemes? I cursed the insidious transnational seductiveness of our lumpen degenerate pop-sub culture, and how it corrupts even the noble savages of desert wadis, on behalf of whose liberation Sissy lost her one and only lust object.

In fact, however, it turns out these Relic Amalekites are native speakers of their own special hand-yammer dialect, natural-born experts at using fingers like tongues. (I mean in the unerotic way.) The phrase "natural-born" is here used in both the literal and synechdochic senses, as I learned from perusing a tract by Blurt Vomitgut on the subject—

male Relic Amalekite with mating crest
engorged: a natural-born expert at using
fingers like tongues

They have no tongues, these former creepers along the gummy sands of the Middling Orient. Nor have they any throats at all, much less the bitubular vocal tract that enables audible speech in upper mammaloid forms.

If I were susceptible to the Darwinizers' schismatic hissings, I might wonder if the somatic energy conserved by such otorhinolaryngologistic shortages was expressed, in the males, in their elaborate and tasteless mating crests.

Perhaps this peculiar state of somatic affairs has something deoxyribonucleically to do with the enriched choco-covered plutonium shells that crackle and squeak from the styro-peanuts our Sovereign Theocracy has with such sarcastic magnanimity heli-crapped on them in Care Packages ever since the promulgation of the genocide policy.

The refugeniks' default manual manner of "speech," so to speak, combined with certain personal hygiene customs different from our own (which I shudder to specify), has caused a cruel aphorism to gain worldwide currency. It has been aptly remarked that, in the Middling Orient (and now, in our backyard as well)—

all talk
is dirty talk

The only question is how in the world they managed to whisper their dirty nothings into Hildegard's deafened eye sockets. Was some false religio-magic involved? Did their peculiar trans-Judeuphratic god supply them with cross-species telepathy? These questions may forever remain exotic mysteries.

Speaking of doing dirtiness with the hands, I suppose you've been wondering how long I was going to put off discussing–

XV.

maestrobation

You search in vain
beneath your sheets for shame.
Peek instead
at sheetrock overhead.
                    —Blurt Vomitgut

I learned, early and well, not to maestrobate, no matter how many aphrodisiacal Flyblown Fruiting Bodies Bitch Mother makes me gorge in the loosely draped presence of my beloved siblette. No matter how my bedroom wallpaper is swirling and metastasizing up to the ceiling. No matter how seamlessly Mom's quantities of fungus interblend the sensations in the soles of my feet with the tingles in the ridges of my scalp, and every bit of me in between, and regardless of the extent to which my bed sheets are behaving badly as vomit in a bucket.

I believe Mom has no sense of
personal boundaries.

The Relic Amalekites make a big flap about being able to hit the ceiling when they maestrobate. As if they know what a ceiling is. Roofs themselves were exotic enough among these manure-spreading nomads even in the pre-Flamma Manna days, before we flattened every mud hut up and down the far Judeuphrates bank.

Well they may brag, the savages. They don't have their female parent suction-cupped overhead, vocalizing like a howler monkey, more distracting than any number of backyard refugeniks peeking through the house-hole.

The nightmare question is how Mom got the ceiling-hitting idea into her head as something that needed either to be prevented or—horrible thought—participated in. For participation seems to be her intent, as she spreads and gapes up there on the sheetrock.

Her sundry face-holes are multiple bull's-eyes for the initial squirts, which, at our house, it is decreed, must be triple. Mom controls even the staccato of our ejaculo-behaviors, our sub-Sneezes Catastrophic. I believe she has no sense of personal boundaries. She cares little about follow-up dribbles and garment-splotching post-nasal dewdrops—hence the camouflaging subtropical batik patterns on our off-the-shoulder love sarongs. She says dribbles and dewdrops are Dad's department. I have no idea what she means by that. Something cynical, no doubt. I am, after all, half the rope in the tug-o'-war between her and the absent dribbler.

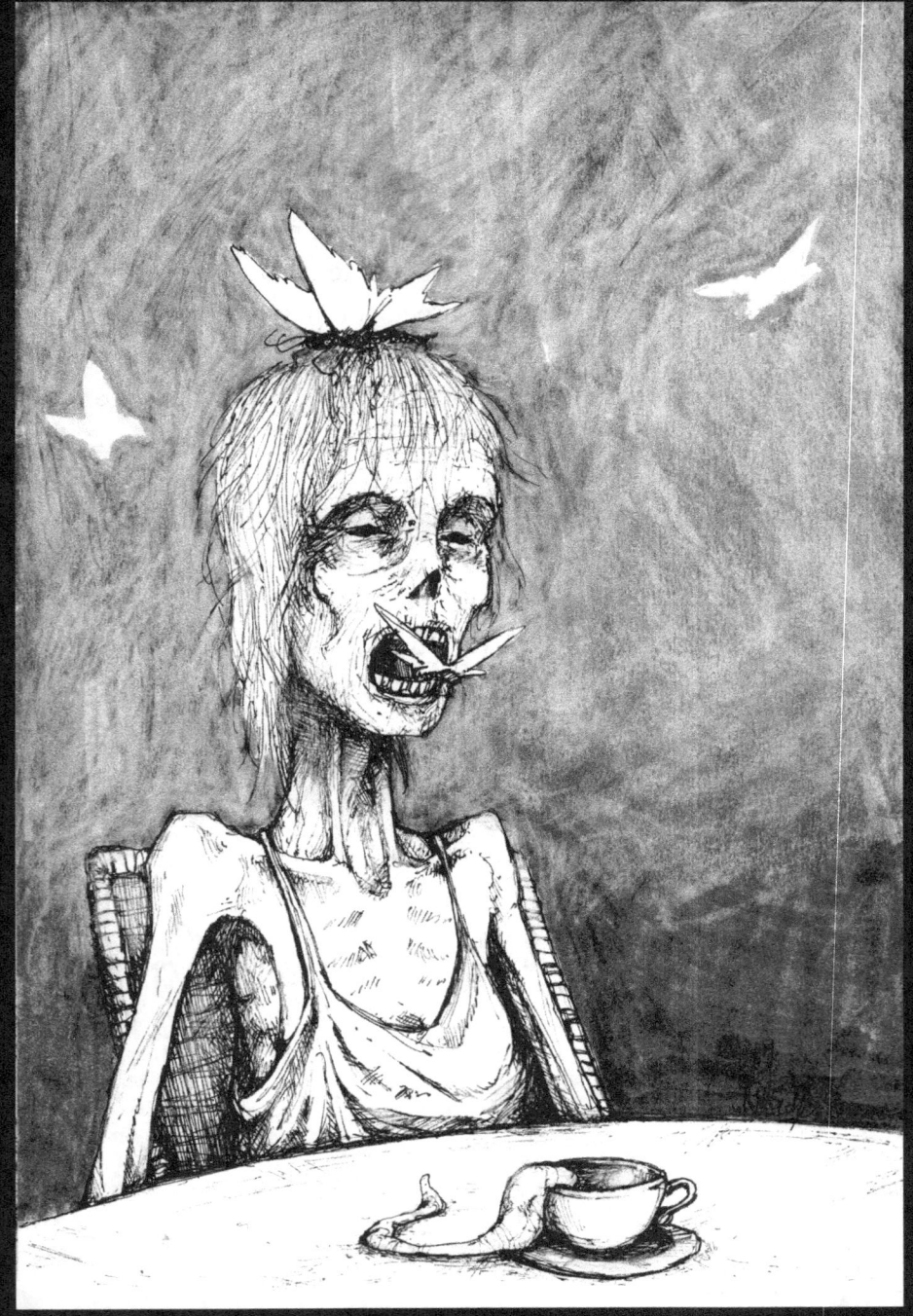

Sissy must ignore the tickles of the minor pathogens. In her condition she cannot afford a Sneeze Catastrophic.

My unfortunate siblette, my notionless little sister, failed to learn the same autoerotic lesson, though much stricter means were employed in her case to cure the maestrobation. This is because, unlike me, being unambiguously gendered, she leans toward congenital lasciviousness, of course.

The less said about my little sibling's explicitly conscious sexuality the better, so allow me to expatiate further upon it.

She once was such a looker. Even Mom seemed to notice. The pathogens she attracted were only the prettiest: petite, pale and pseudo-eyeless. In the name of pudency, Mom allowed both of us to raise our Krystelle Rex-style love-sarongs to off-the-shoulder levels, covering our sundry nipples; but in Sissy's case Mom added straps, modifying the Krystelle Rex look (which is to risk misdemeanor sacrilege). We didn't want anyone other than consecrated men of the spandex penetrating the youngest member of our family before she reached the age of reasoning-with.

Flamma-Manna makes their sweet little
siblettes do the Sneeze Catastrophic.

On the socio-nutrimentality front, Sissy forsook our newfound monophagia and came out as a reform Mahayano-Insectivore. Hence her unwillingness to take in proteins from sentient flutterers and head-alighting pathogens with or without pseudo-eye spots, unless they happened to tumble down onto her lower lip of their own karmic klutziness. However, due to Punjabo-spiritualistic considerations, they must be anesthetized by her halitotic rigmo before surrendering their exoskeletons to her prim incisors.

Sissy doesn't have an eating disorder. She's just small-boned. How many Bruising Betties wouldn't give their left sirloin for such subcutaneous petiteness on the skeletomuscular level?

In my slim siblette, the Sneeze Catastrophic has metastasized to bypass the epiglottis and engage the esophagus as well as the trachea, in the colloquial sense of the Seven-Course Achoo, the Whole-Grain Gesundheit, where one uses a serviette to blow one's nose. As in hemo-bulemia of the bitubular vocal tract.

So, what brought her to this state of affairs? Why, of course, the trauma was—

maestrobation itself

—and the post-trauma as well. She was caught "Rocking the boat," as Bitch Mother euphemizes the way girls do it, which is apparently even rowdier than the methodology of their more or less non-girlish house mates.

Crusty ol' Doc Clyster attempts to cure my sister of maestrobation.

Ol' Doc Clyster, our trusty house-calling Familopath, maintains that self-starved coiffure-shedding femino-juvies suffer from what are medically defined as "paternopenile issues." Our pater is up to his penility in the Styx one must wade to link up with the Relic Amalekites. So I reckon she must instead be pining away for unslaked incest-lust. She hasn't had her innie bred for an under-age.

When the Grand Religiopath and the priestcrafters failed to cure her of crass maestrobation, ol' Doc Clyster was conjured to do a house call. All clad in white, he appeared at her bedroom door like a phosphorescent toadstool, the albino kind that hickeys lightless cave walls.

This time there was no way he could, deliberately or not, misinterpret the word "balls" and misapply his orbit scoop, as the word bore no mention.

XVI.

It took no demonically inspired
crisis of faith...

My dear, tiny, gullible, hopeful siblette's favorite Dad-myth—indeed, the only one she entertains as having an atom of factuality, apart from her self-concocted yarn of backyard interment—is the one that claims he was a blasphemer even before crossing the Judeuphrates, that it took no demonically-induced crisis of faith to drive him to apostasize from the chained and wormy arms of the Divine Krystelle Rex.

No, Sissy believes that, when young, Dad was that rarity of rarities in our Sovereign Theocracy: a home-grown peacenik. If this is true, I can guarantee it was before he met Mom; she'd disturb the peace of a corpse.

According to this (let's speak frankly) ludicrous legend, Dad was forcibly cured of pacifism's civil abomination by the very same trio of certified State Priestcrafters whom later would not so much fail to cure as fail to cauterize his only daughter of maestrobation. Dad was shown, by means of the Grand Religiopath's lingual intrusiveness, the error of his ways. The same priestly organ which cunnilinguated his daughter's civil/sacral strappado penetrated his brain via the left auditory meatus.

To this day, they say, my non-egg-bearing parent wears on his person the stigma of his error like a scarlet letter copied phonetically from an obsolete paleo-alphabet. Talk about tattoo regret: trendy unblood-lust outpacing subcutaneous discolor.

It is murmured about the riverside megalopolis that the Grand Religiopath, having tongued literally thousands of sinful orifices, tasted something extraordinary in Dad's cerumen. And this highest of High Functionaries, like a dog with its first taste of blood, still lives for the day he can find time off his busy schedule cunni-strappadoing citizens' siblettes to wade the Judeuphrates, personally, and finish the meal he started so long ago. If this is his plan, it will be a chase to remember—assuming he doesn't meet Dad wading the other way. Our old man's due for a homecoming. Rather, the homecoming.

While I have no doubt the Grand Religiopath likes the taste of earwax (probably his own best of all), I find my mental eye unable to maintain an image of Dad as peacenik. However, this is not to say I don't hold in common with Sissy a number of other brain scenes featuring her "papa."

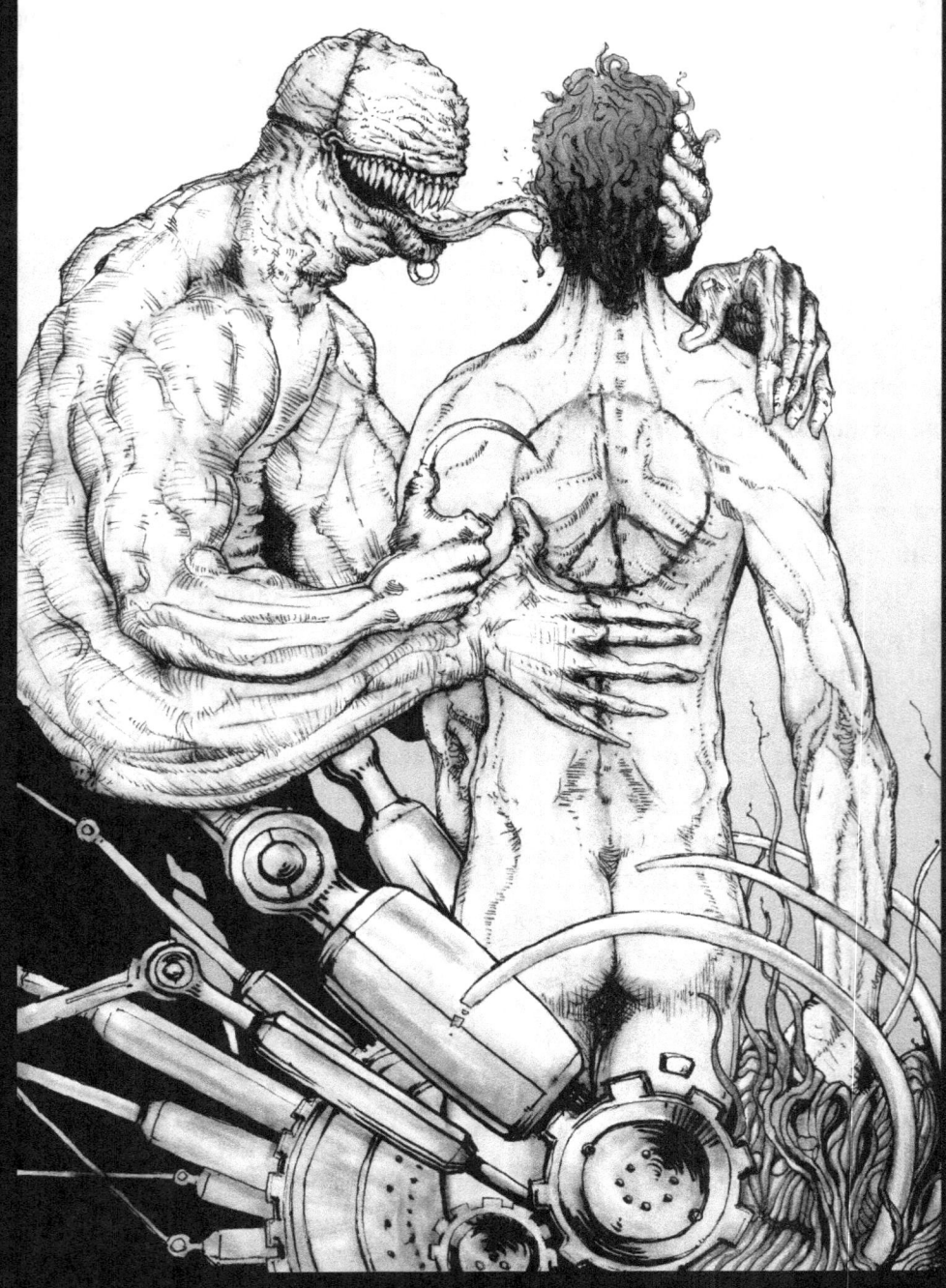

The Grand Religiopath
cures Dad of peacenikism.

Like most neurotically cloistered siblings enslaved to a power-crazed, hypersexualized mom, Sissy and I share identically unwholesome daydreams and quasi-incestuous head visitations, without knowing which of us thought what part first, and whose sense organs were originally engaged, and via the insidious agency of which pathogen they were vectored between us. I'll presently cite one particular fantasy-memory of Dad as an example.

The powerful scrotum-wielding figure in most of our shared dream images prefers to keep his trouseredness ambiguous. Sissy can't bring herself completely to expose the patriarcho-schwanz for which she nurses such a damaged brain-suffusing letch. But it is plenty titillating for a congenitally lascivious daughter to imagine Papa sunken up to his upper pube-line in saline solution which hovers, in the temperature department, between balmy and clammy. "Amniotic" is an adjective that springs to mind.

This time it's not fetal me awash and grinning in the warmish, gritty fluid. Our father is fording, keeping the sandy water at the same pubis level to which Krystelle Rex's tormentors rolled down the sacred love-sarong.

And here's where our mutual infantile memory of him gets fuzzy, or, rather, fluid: we recall a sluggish river. At least the ambient element reconstitutes itself in the back of our heads as vaguely riverine. But I can't be sure. There is something odd about this accumulation of fluid.

I suspect this body of water is materno-wombular, and we are viewing him from an in-utero proto-memory, and therefore our parents must have facio-sexuated while we were yet embellied, and we somehow survived such preemie deep-throating.

"If so," marvels Sissy at my bold suggestion, "Papa must have the muscliest, most upper-horned pecksniff in all counter-zoology!

His face remains strangely unseeable behind his tumescent mating/mayhem crest, and his general tenor remains anabolically steroidal, as though only a featureless mass of sinew and brawn could be imagined tangling fruitfully with a gorgon like Mom.

Horned as a desert patriarch, Dad negotiates the Judeuphrates. And he is being observed from a high cliff on this side. The eyes that lick him like tongues belong to The Grand Religiopath, who has finally found some time off his busy schedule, and the pair of them are about to meet again.

If the Judeuphrates is Dad's amniotic element, then the Relic Amalekite cavalry must be his true vocation. Just as I was chased by Mom's aborto-pathogen, he is hounded by Sovereign Theocratic mercenaries—sorry, contractors.

Mating/mayhem crest in full tumescence,
Dad wades the Judeuphrates.

I say to my little sister, "Maybe our parent wades sub-waist deep due to scrotal shame. He's bracing himself for the embarrassing end which the priestcrafters have planned for him: the rolling-down of his love-sarong to pubis level."

You could with justification expect me to go off and search for him, in the usual way of regular unambiguously scrotal youth: a boilerplate Pa quest. And you might also be canny enough to infer something idiosyncratic about my genetic makeup from the fact that I intend wasting nary a page of this romance searching for anyone, least of all a Darwinistic parent, male, female or hermaphrodite.

xvii.

When the seasons change, the time rolls around for the Relic Amalekites' feathers to fall and adhere to their turds, as though the latter were humiliating clots of tar smeared on a disgraced politician, our backyard being the rail he's run out of town on.

While foraging in metamorpho-molting season, I must scoop aside vast complications of plumes from our sustenance. I can't help but think of Father laying his presumably weary exile's head to rest on foreign soil. And I wonder if his hosts' sheddings are downy enough to pillow his left ear-hole where the "Grand Religio-fucking-asshole-path" tongue-rasped it.

Unfeathered, the refugeniks' offputting shoulder dentition and upper carapaces come into view. You'd think molting would make them look somewhat more mammaloid, but it has the opposite effect. One can only wonder why their strange scribbling god, the so-called Jawhey, made them that way, and gave them such an inefficient method of chit-chat.

The question remains on the table: how did these signifying refugeniks, with their entirely visual means of communication, not only get through to, but win the allegiance of our retina-challenged attack beast, namely Hildegarde von Bingo, she of the scooped orbits?

Every day, more than a couple of times, I ask myself that question while dropping down from the dining room windowsill and facing my supercilious, snooty cyno-pet. And a superstitious suspicion inevitably follows: that Hildegard von Bingo's mute seducers might have been endowed with something like cross-species telepathy by their particular idiosyncratic creator—

Jawhey
the Stylus God

—who wrote and, having written, relieved his botched creations of that chore. That's why they use hand signs and have no paper (a deficiency, as you shall see, with hygienic consequences). The spoken word bears the onerous logos no less than the written.

The Relic Amalekites are the self-styled Originally Selected Beings of this particular god, whom they adore and reverence as the Unitary Executive and Decider of the Present Solar Clump.

He sounds to me like more of a brain lesion symptom than a transcendent being, but nevertheless he's officially adored and reverenced, also, by our dad's turncoat/ apostate heart. Our male parent is, at least technically, a convert. Therefore, if he weren't just trying to be funny galloping under Jawhey's banner, he'd be a mortal enemy of our own national faith.

Transcribed below is some of the differentially fonted promo material which undercover cells of espio-proselytizers attach to utility poles late at night:

Chief Deity of the Relic Amalekites

In the septafold naves of his cathedralic heart, Jawhey suppurates a special letch for Relic Amalekites.

It is said that with each stroke of his chthonian pen he stabs a time-louse on your life scalp, thus numbering your evanescence in this particular niggling solar clump.

Disinterest is his rule. The appearance of a mad cackle is only lent by an accident of connective tissue deployment.

an Ur-Self being torn apart

It is said the Relic Amalekites themselves boasted such a physiognomy, before doing their equivalent of lapsing (which I'd rather not imagine, if you don't mind).

It sounds as though this poor old god, too, like me, was only semi-aborted, early in this cosmic day, pinched between the raggedy hemorrhoids of the Big Emanation—or so converts (like, presumably, Dad) are schooled.

Some blasphemers insinuate that our Sovereign Theocracy's own Krystelle Rex is nothing other than the sibling of the god who presides over Middling Orient—whose environs and inhabitants we presently happen to be debiologizing. Some say our god is just a modification of that earlier entity, yet still the immortal mortal enemy of Jawhey, his fraternal twin. Hence the Divine Krystelle Rex's need of a bloated bureaucracy staffed by clerical apparatchiks and bossed by a Grand Religiopath, and an army capable of bio-genocide. If true, our family exemplifies the split. Dad has gone over to the service of the latter while we continue to truckle under the sway of the former.

Some believe that the state of war between our two regions is nothing less than an Ur-Self being torn apart, the macrocosmic soul depriving itself of integrity, and that Krystelle Rex is one and the same as Jawhey, and that the influx of refugeniks into our municipality is an attempt at racial individuation, and that we are, in fact, cousins to the strange Relic Amalekites. It's a backyard family reunion, minus potato salad.

The divine Krystelle Rex
tends to overcompensate.

Dad explains much of this in his secret letters to me. He writes that our god (his, too, pre-apostasy/desertion) is just an effete version of the grand desert deity. And "Miss Kryssie's" pitiable, chained, handless condition demands the overcompensation of a vast Sovereign Theocracy, underpinned by a warrior caste capable of waging industrialized war, and a cowering corps of priestcrafter-apparatchiks who not only impose Krystelle Rex's will, but pull straight from their sacerdotal asses the very content of that will.

Meanwhile, Jawhey, the original version, the source of wimpily cloned, pullulated wart-growth Krystelle Rex (surname pinned on with unconscious irony), presides over simple preliterate, almost prelingual nomads who don't even wear trousers, as far as anyone can ascertain—apart from their insurgent cavalry (for obvious reasons).

Our current attack upon the Relic Amalekites is therefore autoimmune, like the half-hatched seed, or perhaps the asexually grunted outgrowth, the merely non-girlish first born (like me), impinging upon the territory of the autochthonous rightful tutelary. Our ignorant armies stomp through Jawhey's backyard the same way I tiptoe among the Relic Amalekites' droppings. And our priestcrafters are slanderously demonizing them the same way little sister hallucinates them pincered and suction-cupped and slithering around our dining room window.

more, and less, to the divine Krystelle Rex
than meets the eye...

On several levels, then, it's a question of who in our family forsook whom. If we are, as Dad insinuates in his letters to me, indeed cousins to the Relic Amalekites, see how doubly deep the tragedy of Little Sissy's delusion sinks. She harbors these inaccurate images of her own kin as so different and dangerous, protean as they are delusory.

XVIII.

Okay, so I am willing to entertain a certain grudging admiration for Jawhey, the big snaggle-puss Rival in the Sky. But it's difficult to credit him with endowing his cultists with trans-species telepathy. Worldly war and bio-genocide are middlingly important theodices; but the real head-burner is this:

If it's not the extra-sensory providence of Jawhey, then via what organ could the refugeniks have persuaded my pet not to be nice to me? Might the answer be found in a sense which sinks at the opposite extreme of the spectrum from something so elevated as the sixth, the ethereal, the divine one? Conscious as we are of the Sneeze Catastrophic, should we be probing Hildegarde von Bingo's (let's speak frankly) over-extended snout?

Confessors of the Crypto-Darwinizer heresy have been heard, in back alleys, to mutter under their halitosis about this very topic. They say that, having nose structures somewhat lengthier than our own, this particular species of pet sprouts extra numbers of stench receptors, the kind that are left bare when we succumb to the Sneeze Catastrophic.

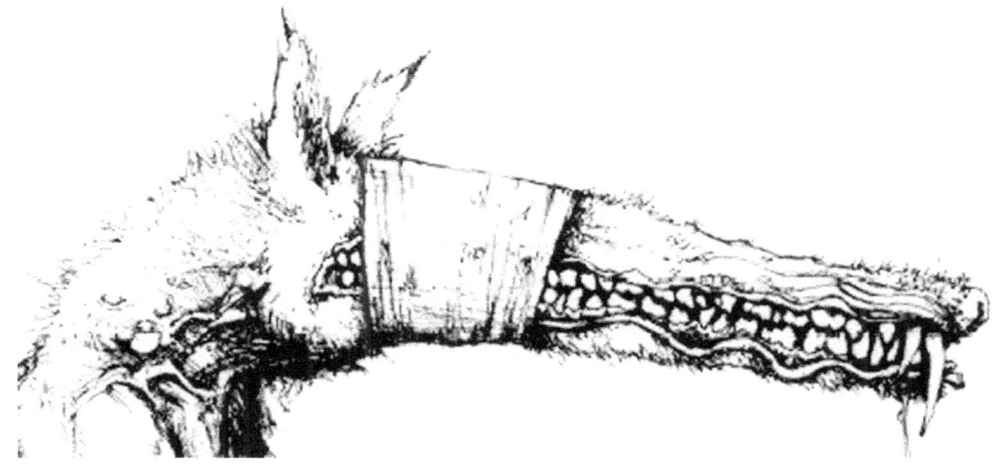

nasal nodes more than sufficient...

Like bat-sonar pinpointing a blood-succulent mosquito twenty feet away on a moonless night, these nasal nodes are more than sufficient to detect subtle yet lexical posturings of deaf-mute digits, provided the latter exude an idiosyncratic odor of their own.

Might, for some odd reason, the Relic Amalekites' grasping, scratching, maestrobating, chattering organs carry some sort of aroma that appeals to natures even more brutish than theirs? How else could they capture the attention, much less the loyalty, of our familo-pet, blind as Lady Justice herself, and teach her to signify like a Talibanger? It's not for lack of comprehension Hildegard of Bingo neglects to bark off the snickers hurled through the dining room window by the very entities against whom she was bred and purchased to protect me, her rightful master.

It remains a mystery from the Middlingly Mysterious Orient. As such, it's a cause for Mom to induce immune system anxiety in us.

Not surprisingly, my pathogen-minded Mom tells me to stay away from the followers of Jawhey, not due to their religio-politics, but simply because they are from across the river and their hands probably smell weird in some way imperceptible to other than cyno-snouts.

The Other has pathogens that can alight on you. Except when performing my nutritional chore, I should stay out of the backyard and remain in the dining room being raped of my life sauce by Mom, because these outlanders will cause differentially evolved outlander pathogen species to alight on me and make me do the Sneeze Catastrophic, and I might even pass the deathliness on to my little siblette.

differentially evolved
outlander pathogen species

XIX.

Obsessive-compulsive fear of
the Sneeze Catastrophic

So, have Mom and I instilled an obsessive-compulsive fear of the Sneeze Catastrophic in you yet? Congratulations. Dry-heaving phobias temper the abs and make you more attractive when autopsy time rolls around.

Speaking of which, there is contagion on these pages. There's a flu to make the bubonic plague look like diaper rash, to make Flamma-Manna look like annealing balm for that rash. If I were Bitch Mother, I would have so many warnings for you at this late stage that you might hesitate to turn the page, to peel back the lids on this gawker. I would, for your own good, make you feel like a helpless, repugnant, small creature fastened to an eyeball with a chain more adamantine than those which transfixed the Divine Krystelle Rex's elbows.

Depending on your state of soul-preparedness, this family romance could turn out to be like a spell in the most horrific of all torture chambers. The famous rat cage just might get muzzled to your kisser—except you're the rodent, and you've been hampered with a predisposition to rabies. And a membrane has metastasized along your finger bones where the Mom-pathogens have taken control and secreted sheet tumors.

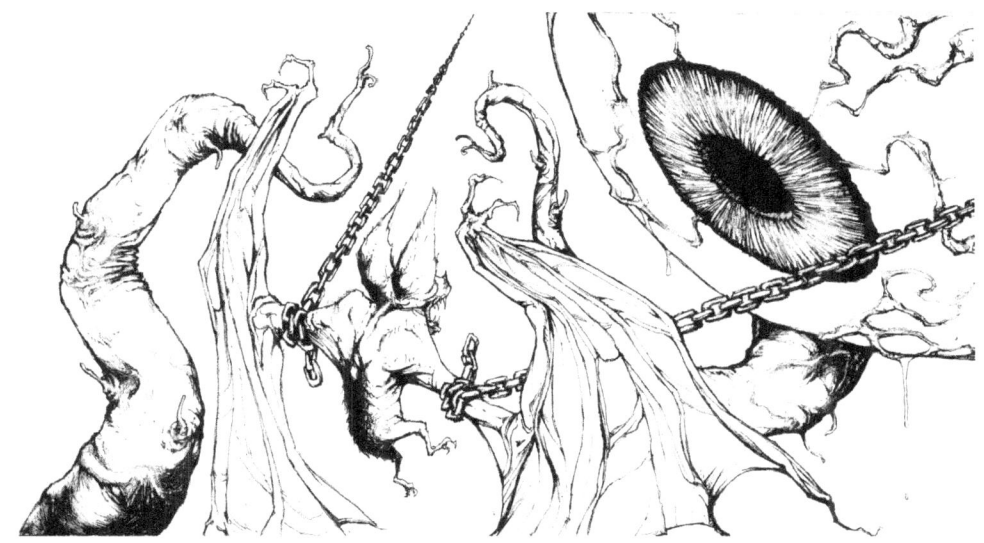

You're the rodent...

But this does not mean you need fret about having picked up a pathogen and passing it on. You don't lack permission to commence considering this family romance with a sneeze. Go ahead and hurricane hard enough to blow back this page. Phlegm-paste it flat against the previous. Take a peek through the eyeballs you just atomized in a coarse red shpritz among the tantalizing tints.

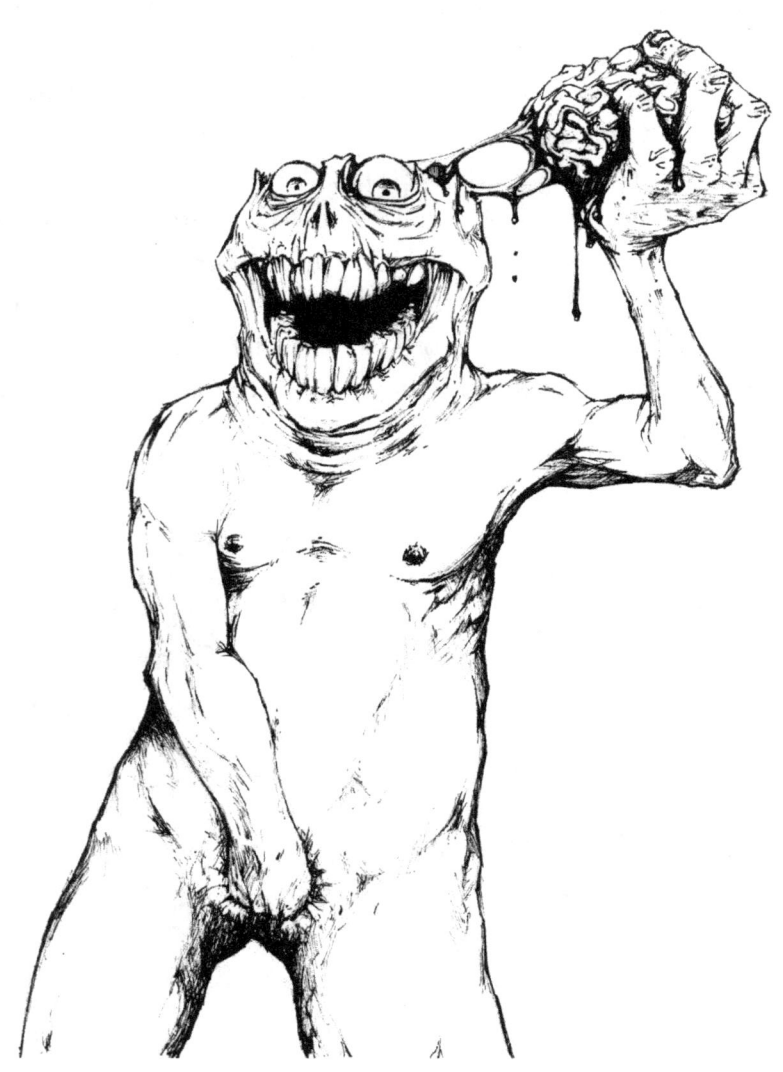

Prefix abuse with self-.

An eight- to twelve-hour introspection is indicated at this point. You know, the kind you get sucked into after being sent to your room—not without, but, worse—with your dinner. And you've not been issued the usual personified tallow invigilator to distract the notional flooding that accompanies any unlit bedtime in such a household. It would amount to child abuse if you didn't get there first and prefix the abuse with self-.

But first, before moving any further into this proposition that is shuffled in so many layers between your fingers, it is recommended that you pause a moment and look inside the stacked deck called yourself. There could be something far worse than a mere prettified Mom-bug mired in the inky condiments of this cellulose sandwich. It could be waiting to be picked up, not by your sinuses or extremities, but by your soul. An immaterial pathogen, so to speak.

When you've been persuaded to eat way too many holy eucharist shaman mush-bowls, prepared by a not so much over-anxious as sadistic mom, a hyper-religiose parent who tries to conceal her perfidy under a veneer of 'shroom piety—you often wind up mired in those hellish eight-to-twelve-hour entheospections, those states of neuro-toxicity that make you understand why your melanin-challenged ancestors were traditional mycophobes, those moods that admit no border between what you see and what you'd give anything to unthink about what you can't bear to look at.

Think all the way down to...

Such is the permanent post-prandial mood at our house—except inside Mom's own head, of course. Her inner pugnacity is such as to render the hugest, most crawling Relic Amalekite turd-growth to nothing more than a dandelion fluff against an eyelid. Her vitality dissolves us, embosoming entheogenicity itself, like vitriol buttering an unleavened wafer, and she's perma-cheery, eyes, mind and, especially, mouth wide open.

Are you ready for that? Stroke your head and think deep into the tentacled core of your subcranial colloids. Are you really prepared to engage your eyeballs so deeply with what you hold in your hands at this moment, until you think all the way down to—

the Relic Amalekites' personal hygiene?

XX.

I don't want this to degenerate into a speciesist tract, but the whisper-snickered tattles about these ethno-types eating with their faces and wiping their assholes with both hands must contain a kernel, or maybe an undigested peanut, of truth.

This idiosyncratic state of personal-hygienic affairs has a direct bearing on why our backyard's mini-ecosystem is peculiarly suited to this relgio-ethnicity, and why they migrated here in such numbers in the first place.

Like the paleolithic-style wretches they were when originally condemned to total species-expungement in splatter-porno-scriptural days, they remain hunter-gatherers at core. (Though, come to think of it, from what position do I condescend, having been reduced to that level myself, or at least the latter half of the job description?) Their proud yet squalidly nomadic culture never invented anything like an alphabet, so paper never entered their so-called "minds." Therefore, neither did that superfluous luxuriance of civilization come near their opposite ends.

Can it truly be called a crotch?

So they require handfuls of greenery to be perpetually poised at the ready, tickling up between their struthious legs, to aid in the two-fisted de-chunkification of their uniquely configured fundaments after evacuation of whatever unimaginable bowel apparatus their Jawhey, himself indifferently configured, has bothered to plumb for them by way of a crotch-vent. Sometimes, as I ponder our foreign guests from a few paces off, I wonder if they can truly be said to have crotches any more than oral cavities.

This has resulted in the famously exotic custom, which is known abroad as the—

Middlingly Oriental Grass Wipe

It has come popularly to symbolize their entire presence on the planet, just as kindergartens full of type-two diabetics stereotypify a certain other civilization which will remain nameless.

The on-the-hoof running grass-wipe is doubly piquant as a behavior because, back across the river in the occupied territories of their home-sand, even before we smote them and our Flamma-Manna settled whitely down to liquefy the olive skins of their siblettes, stands of grass were as few and far-flung as oases. Now we have debiologized the place, the above statement can be made even more emphatically.

So, where they've lived for seven thousand years, the chance to wipe one's ass has always been a real treat, the equivalent of stumbling upon a stand of date palms in the middle of a hypoglycemic jag. Finding themselves heli-dumped charitably down to a backyard grassy as ours, our foreign guests believe they've been translated whole to their monotheistic heaven and laved in 600 houris' copulation sauces, without even suiciding for the privilege.

This marvelously pullulizing expression of carbon not only promotes the growth of the Flyblown Fruiting Body at home, but it brings forth the occasional marvel of life on the otherwise hermetically sterile sands of the far Judeuphrates bank. The Amalekite ethnicity truly is autochthonous, one with its native soil, for there would literally be no soil without them. To the irreligious, the crypto-Darwininst, it would no doubt reduce to a chicken-egg paradox.

Everyone else will begin to see, on pondering the purity of this symbiosis, the depth and extent of Our Theocracy's crime. We have been destructive to a source of calories as well as clean crotches. We have violated nature, nutrition and hygiene as

the riverside where they've roamed
for seven thousand years...

well. Dad—who, in his youth, helped hawk our weapon in this felony—is attempting to atone by riding at the head of their mounted resistance, doomed as it is.

Nomads prematurely introduced to the sedentary existence of the municipality put on weight and become louche. They succumb to luxuriation and become decadent and socially graceless. With the corruption of civil lawns comes inclemency of speech and ingratitude toward the host. Hence their mean mitt wiggles, which our pet was purchased to bark off. The Relic Amalekite chicks, in particular, are always signing something bitchy to me.

Their handed babble, though produced by the opposable thumb that only we amongst higher primates possess as a non-Flamma Manna-induced mutation, are grammatically and lexically quaint, as they are influenced by the hiatally belched cretino-rhythm of our Sovereign Theocracy's own disaffected youth bangers. As I try to scrape up a few calories for my family I am rapped with such poetry as—

"Look with derisive laughter upon the litter-runt who in probability conceals a vulva homologue under the strapless prom gown which is inappropriately effeminate."

a few flecks of connective tissue
on the dining room rug

"Scorn with cruelty the sister boy's beehive hair stylings, complete with insect life. He no doubt maestrobates."

The stinkingest garbage of our culture oozes through our porous borders and osmoses across the monotidal oceans that protect us but nobody else. Backyard refugeniks embrace melano-gang couture, but disdain Mom's love-sarongs and mock them when they appear off my shoulders. I take this as nothing other than a warm recommendation. Her aesthetic is far too refined to filter down to third-world migrant grass wipers. They scoffed, too, at her feather boa.

This in spite of the fact that I water down my 'do and switch to dungarees before going out to scavenge familial subsistence, and rarely, if ever, maestrobate in within their shot. This indicates to me that the wretches have been not only peeking, but listening and, ominously enough, comprehending through the aperture of that particular blind sac in our house-bowel called the "dining room"—ironically enough, for that's where Mom drains life from my siblette and is trying to consume soul nutrition off me as well.

And it turns out that these Middlingly Oriental Grass Wipers employ not the postures so much as the rich, ripe, fecal miasma of their fingers. Theirs is a stench phonetics. Being animalistic themselves, the refugeniks have been able to use, not their hand chatter so much as their hand stink, eloquently enough to turn Hildegard von Bingo's elongated head with silent middlingly oriental schmooze talk.

So I have no affectionate pet to commiserate with, to help me release my pressure, to postpone the love explosion I earlier spoke of, which will end with either me or Mom getting metabolized, with perhaps a few flecks of connective tissue on the dining room rug. This romance in your hands may yet end like that, because I get no red steam release from my slippages out the dining room window.

XXI.

In my barely beyond fetal, half-hatched, irrecovered memory I contain a vague image of The Father Figure riding off into a dioxin-discolored sunset, or maybe dawn. He's ill-defined, a more or less apocalyptoid figure on a vintage ride, his mating/mayhem crest contracted to conform to the aerodynamics of a cavalry canter, seen from a distance hazed with motherly lies, unrequited daughterly embryo-lust and, of course, the blood-tinted religio-patriotic outrage of our Sovereign Theocracymen, in the lethal person of the Grand Religiopath.

As per our Divinely Revealed Criminal Code, on a charge of blasphemo-treason in time of transriverine genocide, the priestcrafters would like nothing better than to drag this parent of mine home, slit his belly just a tad, unspool his entrails through the tight hole, anoint them with holy astringent, then wrap them, love-sarong-wise, to pucker and contract around his neck in the sun—assuming a glint or two of the latter resource can be persuaded to peek between billows of our Sovereign Theocracy's proud smog.

Though our religion, race, nation, tribe, culture, language and landmass are coextensively coterminous, and though qualification for our citizenship is neither more nor less than chromosomal, the influx of refugeniks and their mushroom-friendly excrement, scented with such sheer alienness, has filled our bellies, cross-fertilizing us, like Melanogroids fetching their muscled bongos northward to vitalize the effete medleys of the Carcinomians.

Hence, I suppose it's possible to recognize the poetic justice of the execution method proposed for turncoats like Dad, when the coat they turn is made of their, and our, literal skin. Since oneself is being forsaken in every sense of the word, why not be throttled by one's own innards?

I undergo this very punishment in bimonthly dreams which surprise me with their solidarity for someone I have never, and will never meet. Like pendulum clockwork, I drape myself in Father's love-sarong.

Here is the real reason why we eat off the soil of our own yard. It's too miserable in the grocery store. To the greater world of the riverside megalopolis we are nothing more or less than the grotesque detritus of a heretic/deserter who helps idolatrous infidels riot obstreperously somewhere foreign.

I drape myself in my father's love-sarong.

A loyal member of our family (if there was one) would be obliged to point out to these neighborhood gossips that, according to the revealed Relic Amalekite porno/scriptures, Jawhey personally unrolled that river and its banks in one of the Twelve Days of Creation to be their rightful perma-turf, not a proving ground for our latest murder products.

Although, if that is the case, and if this ostensible Jawhey is also responsible for having created the configuration of their fundamental vents, one wonders why he didn't supply the soil underfoot with more plentiful provender for the Middlingly Oriental Grass Wipe.

I can offer you an exercise if you want to gauge their intellectual capacities. Try explaining to them that their pcd of refugeniks just happened to be heli-deposited into the backyard of a household whose former head is at this moment selflessly attempting to win them back their home-sand, thereby condemning himself either to perpetual exile or to execution. Try pointing out to these refugeniks that Dad crossed their precious ancestral Judeuphrates to link up with their coreligionists' resistance (measly as it is), and they should be worshipful toward us rather than getting all snickery when looking and listenting in upon our dining room.

I invite you to gauge their facial expressions when being informed of this shameful irony. None whatsoever.

XXii.

There is a third sex
among the Relic Amalekites.

In my foraging mode, as I tiptoe among the refugeniks unobtrusively as possible to gather our familistic breakfast, lunch, sacramental snack, and dinner, I always worry they're about to grab me with their dirty-talking hands, and call me a certain two-syllable bad name that gets under my skin more effectively than the worst Mom bug.

There is a third sex amongst our backyard squatters, which I call The Jocks, for lack of a better name. At rest they are indistinguishable from the females. But, under duress or sadistic excitement, also during the metamorpho-molting season, they are peculiarly adapted, in the name of dissimulation and camouflage, to retract their shoulder teeth and suck in the trilobite shells which define their species. These structures, upon retraction, pucker into a roughly prosimian physiognomy, like a Mom-style pathogen with its falsely eye-spotted wings. A sort of headlike knob is just incidentally formed by the wads and folds of puckered exoskeleton, upon which, as if in some dim bestial mimicry of the mating/mayhem crest displayed by higher species, they will plop the latest chapeau from a Talibanger boutique in one of the riverside megalopolis malls.

It's a form of aping worthy of an illuminated panel in the crypto-Darwinizer's black-magical bestiary. At these times they come uncannily to resemble the worst pathogen Mom herself ever hallucinated and sicced upon our coiffures, as if in her mock-maternal sado-anxiety she was actually trying to teach us a geopolitical hypochondria. The disorder they induce with their pathogenic digits is rupture of the sclera, the goosing of the retina.

Through their provisional mouthish mimesis they are able, like parrots, more or less mindlessly to mimic speech, but no more than a couple of syllables per mouthful. Under such quasi-linguifying metamorphoses their fingers are freed up for more emphatic forms of ideational transfer.

Their peculiar grass-wiped uncrotchedness remains as a telltale sign that no true transpeciation has occurred, only the dissembling of the octopus or chameleon, with their anal vents staying in place at the base of what would be the sternum, were these creatures equipped with rib cages in the first place.

the worst pathogen Mom ever hallucinated

The list of primitive tricks these backyard bullies learned from our Sovereign Theocracy's disaffected melano-youth includes, when they want to express particularly emphatic notions, the use of the middle and forefingers as eyeball gougers. All I can say is tighten your eyelids like sphincters in a locker room.

This is called the internationalization of culture, and we have been instructed to take pride in it, as our Sovereign Theocracy is a Fondue Pot for all manner of miscegeno-cheesiness. Anyone whose home-sand we occupy and render uninhabitable is welcome to relocate here and enjoy sub-citizen status, assuming they survive the Flamma-Manna which we cause to fall on their "corrupt dictators"— which is what we call any tribal elders, sacerdotal authorities, grandmas, etc., who happen to enjoy bigger than average palm-frond huts.

The Relic Amalekites call me a certain bad name which, given the precise nature of my hereditary hypochondria and lifelong dietary behavior, could not be better calculated to grate on my soul like ragged fingernails on a Flamma-Manna blister. It won't be repeated here, this epithetic hideosity. But when I slip into their midst these bad imitation Talibangers call me out, as follows:

"You're not bearing much resemblance to your male parent, are you? Unlike you, he flung off your mama's decolletaged promenade nightie. He fights over the big water to liberate our most antiquated cradle of civics. It appears as though heroism skips a generation in your evolutionary nook."

XXiii.

What can I say? Like most expatriates, they're pathetically out of touch with current events. Have a look at Dad's latest secret letter from the "most antiquated cradle" which our squatting guests couldn't wait to escape—

I'm coming home. I'm wading the river for the second time in my life, now in the opposite direction, unmounted.

I have turned my odd-toed ungulate out to pasture in the sand—a stud if there ever was one, with struts and rivets in addition to the studs.

I no longer need the ride I rode instead of my bride, because—as you well know—I have an ultimate mount waiting on your side of the river, a center of consciousness to centaur myself on to, whom I can depend on, once and for all, forever. Stand by for that, my youngster.

I'm getting old. Just as the backs of patriarchal bonobos get silver, so do the mating/mayhem crests of us aging cavalrymen become permanently engorged, distended at full display. This is a reverse irony, geronto-priapically speaking, a literal yet belated horniness.

Dad's permanent distension.

family / romance

I'm coming to meet that big deadline we all face, yes. But in this case it will come in a final cis-Judeuphratic struggle, a hand-to-hand pugnacity, with none other than the functionary who tongued the peace symbol among my shoulder blades, time gone by, and more recently cunnilingo-strappadoed my youngest spawn: the Grand Religio-fucking-asshole-etcetera.

welcoming party

And guess who observes my father's progress from a cliff on this bank, tongue writhing with anticipation of waxy bouquet. Bolstered, underwired and propped in an especially exacerbated version of the spandex chasuble, it's a welcome-home party of one.

some urban renewal

♦♦♦♦

Dad comes ashore in the same riverside megalopolis that once housed the expo where he met Mom. There has been some urban renewal, rendering the population center and its malls even stranger than they were all those years ago.

trio of State Priestcrafters, plus backup

The Grand Religiopath comes down from his cliff to meet Dad in the urban setting. True to his reputation for honor, the asshole has brought his trio of priestcrafters, plus a backup, stacking the odds.

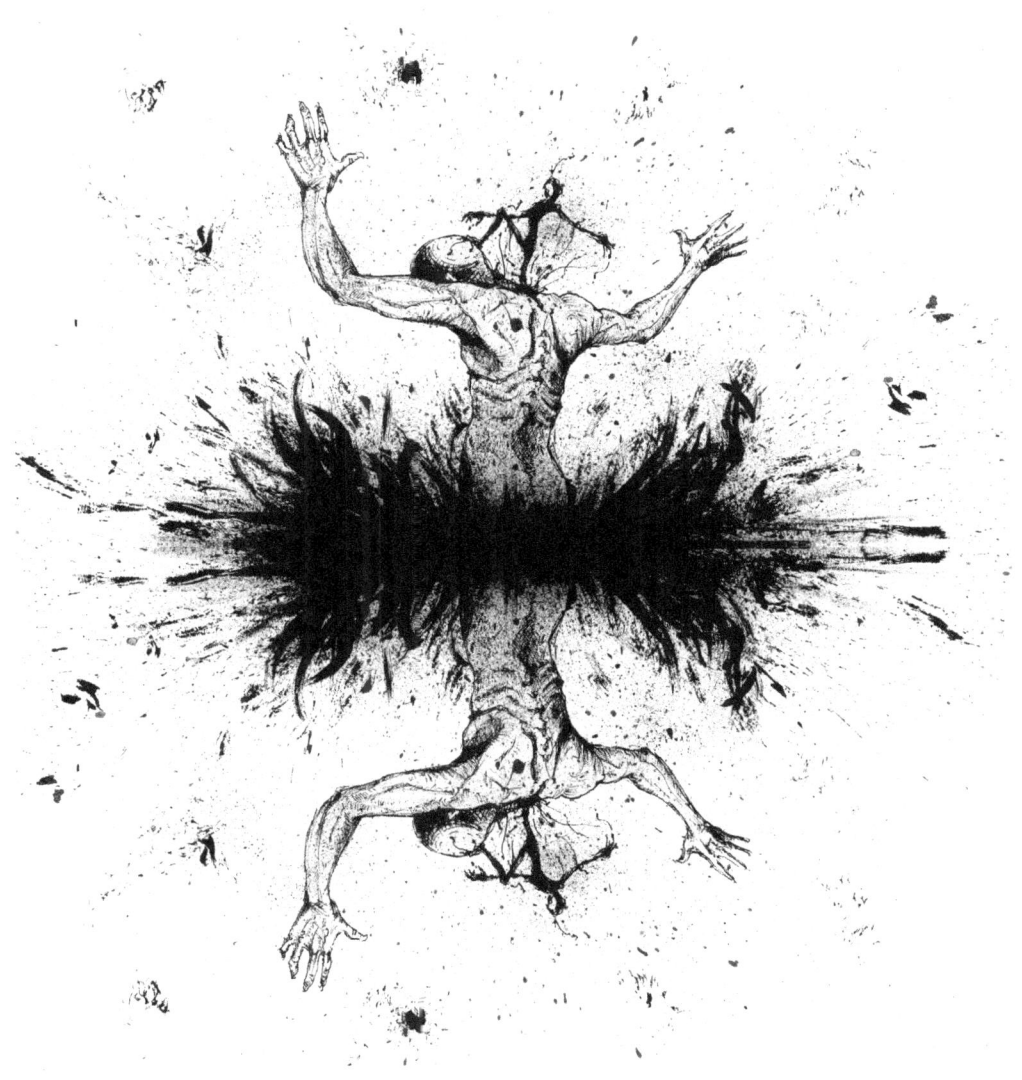

What follows is not so much a struggle as a metabolization.

I wish it were more—I don't know—emotional or something. But I hardly knew the guy.

XXIV.

Talking of religiosity and the One Special Foremost Fear it is supposed to band-aid over, I suppose I have to make it explicit. Our family has experienced limb-loss, ghost pain. Dad is dead. He's a—

dead dad

And I bet, having heard that, you've already guessed it's not just with entomology that Bitch Mother exerts her will on our upper-respiratory tracts. She hijacks our weep-sniffles as well, or what is more sensitively called "the grieving process."

After sulking through an entirely unexpected, yet brief, moment of strange blue catatonia—which I choose to interpret as a distorted form of sadness—she got her dander back up and commenced with the usual bare-naked mycosophic hyper-religiosity. Her way of sublimating spousal bereavement is to go all priestess-crafty on us.

in return for services rendered

family / romance

Dad's homecoming-funeral took place in the backyard. And guess who performed as mourners and pallbearers. I suppose, in their animalistic way, you-know-whom did sincerely consider him a national hero. But I got the impression Mom engaged their services in return for scavenging rights afterward.

Mom went all priestess-crafty on us.

family / romance

Our family has harbored a Cassandra all this time. What appeared, for all these years, merely to be Sissy's schizoid hallucination about Dad bedungeoned in the backyard turned out to be nothing less than time-leaping precognition.

We sank him in the shit of the creatures whose stay-at-home cousins he failed to save from live skeletalization.

Mom's vulvic behavior at the paternal funeral grossed me out, to the extent that, afterwards, I repaired to my room, where (after checking the ceiling for any moms adhering to the sheetrock), I shed my love-sarong and every tonsorial permutation till my scalp was bare as the divine Krystelle Rex's, and I expressed my unhappiness by means of breather-hole.

Do you think the noise might bother Bitch Mother as she lies, bored, yawning, butt-scratching, in her chamber directly overhead? No, she likes it. She calls it "Her offspring practicing his wind instrument instead of the percussion stick for a change."

No, she likes it.

With her pathogens and her monophagia and her shamaness religiosity, she has as good as amputated my hands, Krystelle Rexing me to the wrists, and robbed my ability even to maestrobate in lightlessness. Is it a wonder I howl like a monkey?

Mom's vulvic behavior at Dad's funeral
grossed me out.

I don't think she understands that I am preparing myself for a certain genetic function here.

XXV.

If such a burlesque Dad send-off causes comparatively stable me to howl in my room, it amounts to the cruelest mistreatment of his daughter. She goes all but catatonic to see her worst fears of paternal interment carried out—by her own family, no less.

Then she snaps out of it and becomes irritating. Sissy takes up her dollie-wollies and gambols one too many times around the dining room table, to inexpressibly hideous effect. So Mom gets together with crusty Ol' Doc Clyster, our familistic comic relief, and the two of them determine that my sister constitutes a medical waste disposal problem.

That's her ostensible thinking. But she's obviously concerned that her daughter might not remain in a perpetual state of arrested development. She could respond to this loss with growth, and grown daughters tend to see moms as they truly are, looking them right in the death-bound eye. Mom can't have that, so Doc Clyster must be called in.

Sissy mustn't look Mom in the eye.

Since visiting our home the last time, the doc has coincidentally been pondering that very problem. His head already bursting full with erudition, he has developed an unorthodox technique to ensure that he will never learn from his clinical errors and diagnostic missteps. This also saves money on kerosene and kindling, and is easier on the environment—at least till potty time, which, as with so many of our senior citifieds, rolls around infrequently enough in the doc's case. Besides, recycling body parts and allowing stem cells to land, unsecured, in a dumpster runs contra to the Grand Religiopath's spiritual queasiness.

The Seven-Course Achoo,
the Whole-Grain Gesundheit

So the doc tries it on Sissy, with Mom's blessing and urging. But the child, having been world-class bulemic ever since Winfrey's memorial meal, transmits to him the Seven-Course Achoo, the Whole-Grain Gesundheit pathogen, and is back in a splash.

XXVi.

My suspicions about parthenogenesis have become certainties. The only thing I wonder now is whether there's a seam between us. Was there ever discontinuity between me and my former host twin? Maybe Mom has become the overdue growth on my back which corresponds to the one she herself displays when suiting up for thanato-estrus.

Am I Mom's former wart, an ex-ball of hair and teeth that sprouted like a pus-distended lymph node in the left armpit of her doubly prehensile hump? If so, our virgin relationship would conduce to reabsorption, one parasite turning the tables on the other. She is Abigail to my Britney, my prehensile Hensel.

Parthenogenesis would explain the uncanny control she's always had over me—and my ability, no less uncanny, to turn that around on her and osmose the fluids in reverse, back up the birth-hole. This pertains to the inevitable moment when the yoked pair of us will revert and convert and pervert until she's but a graft on my shapely shoulders—for I am the firstborn of a Cavalry Caste family.

Mom won't stop bleeding over my shoulder.

With our family dysfunctioning all around me in puddles, I try to do a little escapist reading. I attempt to take in Blurt Vomitgut, but the red and black widow tries to distract me. She fears I'll read the true nature of pathogens, in particular that she herself is the virulent one that has lit on me.

I can feel her thighs. She's reading over my shoulder, bleeding over my shoulder, forcing her post-menopausality to blend with the Vomitgut textures. Literacy is a struggle for some folks; integration of the corpus is a struggle for others.

The fresh widow, who should be in her weeds, would appear to be Lady Paramount of this domestic scene; but it's an exchange of body fluids. Some of the sauce is osmosing counter-gravitationally. I dissolve her. This is her death scene, not mine. I am doing a Stephen Daedalus. I whole-head orgasm her off in a Sneeze Megacatastrophic.

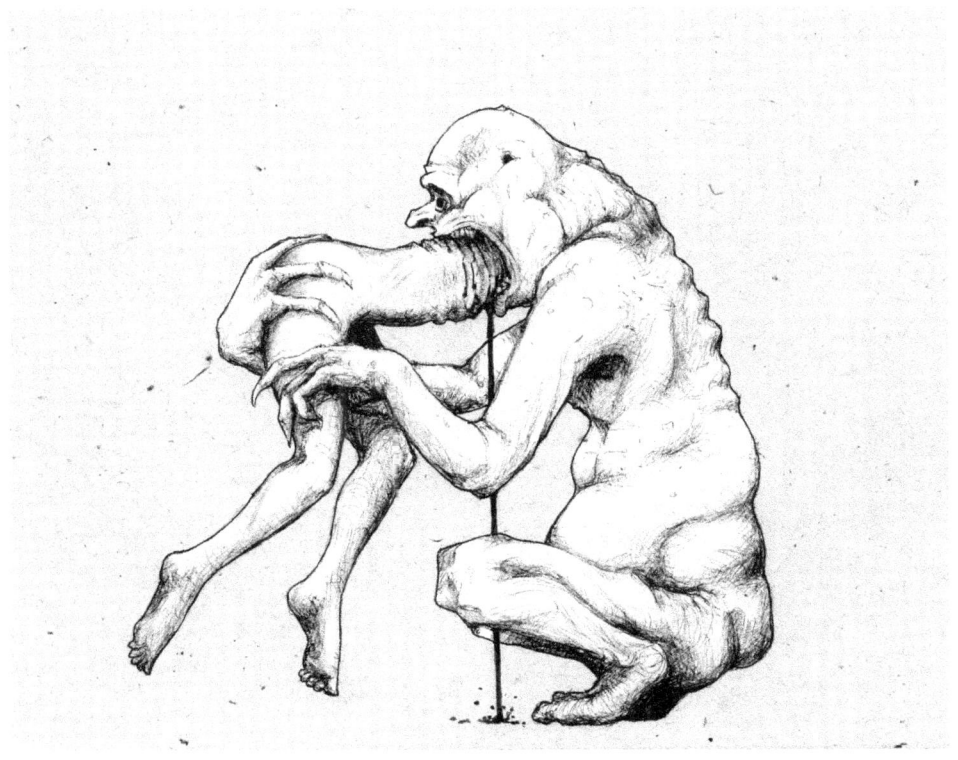

medical waste disposal

When I absorb Mom—or, at any rate, a pretty hefty chunk of her, like a weakened pathogen, it amounts to a kind of incestuous homeopathy. It's only logical for Doc Clyster to make one final house call and dispose of the waste from my self-medication.

XXVii.

Nobody remains in the house but my little siblette and me.

Somewhat risen out of her regressive mode, having shed or maybe eaten her dolly-wolly and grown back much of her scalp filaments, she stands sentry at the dining room window. The refugeniks cannot eavesdrop and mock with their tonguey digits because Sissy, my whole family now, holds them at bay with nothing but her general air of unwholesomeness. Act like a sick spook and they shy away, for they are superstitious.

All other windows have been absorbed like tumors with no blood vessels to feed them. Doors and other domicilic apertures have been atomized, laser-scalpeled away, their holes healed over with patterned cicatrices. All that remains is the wallpaper, the ceilingpaper.

I am displaying my physical and moral subsumption of dead Mom's doubly prehensile hump with dead Dad's inflamed mating/mayhem crest. The latter is looking, not reading, over my shoulder, like a guardian. He rides his eldest offspring with all the cooperative dependency of a crack cavalryman. His postmortem strength is part of me, poised at the ready if required.

holding off the eavesdroppers with nothing
but her general air of unwholesomeness

Thus I have absorbed both parents. I have rolled my love-sarong off the shoulders and down to where it rides like a fluid surface that renders my genital configuration ambiguous, in emulation of Absent Father—to make a river of the garment forced on me by Mom. Yes, it's a skirt, but the Mommishness is made mine. My nakedness is that of a selfless Cavalryman wading the Judeuphrates, a salvific papa pube-deep in backyard dungeon drainage—paralleling the execution garment of Krystelle Rex in throes of iconic passion.

Similarly my hair choice indicates that I have not been enwrapped by Mom, but have contained her. Yes, I sport a fem-'do, but it's my own stylization: the beehive, full of eye-spot pathogens which spread the Sneeze Catastrophic that, in turn, spreads the physiognomy around the room in a black and red mist.

I have teased my hair and put on the finest wrap-around garment in Bitch Mother's dank closet, and my eyes are bound so as not to distract yours with mutual revulso-magnetism. Mom has blinded but not spayed me like a backyard attack-mammaloid. She has caused the wrong pair of balls to be scooped.

Dad rides again.

My head is also tightly bound to keep it from exploding in case I sneeze. Bound with a blindfold around the face, a hovering Saturn-ring around the beehive 'do— the halo that doughnuts my wonderfully restored Mom-coiffure. The expected pathogen has been gutted and transmuted to a mobius tiara. And note the absence of pathogens nesting up there. Healing, disinfection, integration.

I am recollecting emotions in tranquility, leaving an account book to be deposited, buried Qumran-wise, among the evacuated rubbly detritus of our exploded Romantic Family, deep under feathery turds.

It is only when Dad's letters keep arriving that I realize how such lethally seditious mail has been getting through to me. There was no foolhardy or suicidal postman involved. The paternal epistles were my very own hallucinations all along, self-addressed if not stamped. They've been expressions of my own literary bent, my inner Blurt Vomitgut waiting to come to consciousness with Dad's return home in a box. I have blurted and vomited my own guts all along.

Dressed like Krystelle Rex, equipped with stylus like his rival-twin-other self, I have subsumed both halves of the shizo-god, brought integrity to Jawhey and his effete outgrowth. I'm not so much a literary man as a slinger of graphic abstractions via the stylus—in this way I take on the attributes of my trans-Judeuphratic cousins' tutelary. If you want this graphic item to murmur in your right ear, or your left or your inner-, you need to master

some hieroglyphs. Not Chinese or Egyptian, but the kind scraped on hot sandstone cliffs by accident of wind and water. You want the kind of ideo-paleographs that require a wide expanse so they can be silently spoken with a broad sweep.

Observe the never-before-seen yet uncannily familiar calligraphy which I, with a virtuoso flourish of one massive yet delicate hand, beautify the Scroll of Flowing Beauty, this final apotheosis of your narrator as artificer, this—

ekphrastic auto-evocation, this sheer ecstatic hermaphroditic spasm of bimegalomania.

About the Artist

Nick Patterson is a visual artist whose love of twisting minds and turning heads has led him to explore all the darkness the human experience can muster, through high contrast ink drawings. With no official training in the visual medium, Patterson's art is loosely tethered to reality, although it is very detailed. His inspiration is drawn from an amalgam of cartoons, comics, and movies. Carrying a sketchbook with him everywhere, he lets no flicker of imagination escape. Nick Patterson's art has been published in several small magazines and novels. He currently lives in a city full of flowers on the western edge of Canada.

About the Writer

When Tom Bradley was a little boy he was given a gazetteer for Christmas. As little boys will, he looked up all the places in the world that start with the F-word. There were two, Fukien in China and Fukuoka in Japan. Little did he suspect that he would one day be exiled to both. Tom is a former lounge harpist. During his pre-exilic period, he played his own transcriptions of Bach and Debussy in a Salt Lake City synagogue that had been transformed into a pricey watering hole by a nephew of the Shah of Iran. He taught British and American literature to Chinese graduate students in the years leading up to the Tiananmen Square massacre. He was politely invited to leave China after burning a batch of student essays about the democracy movement rather than surrendering them to "the leaders." He wound up teaching conversational skills to freshman dentistry majors in the Japanese "imperial university" where they used to vivisect our bomber pilots and serve their livers raw at festive banquets. But his writing somehow sustains him.

www.ingramcontent.com/pod-product-compliance
Lightning Source LLC
Chambersburg PA
CBHW081227020726
47503CB00011B/2939